$C/3$

W9-BDP-432

BAKER & TAYLOR

The Second Jungle Book

The Second Jungle Book

Rudyard Kipling

WILDSIDE PRESS
Doylestown, Pennsylvania

First published in 1895.

The Second Jungle Book
A publication of
WILDSIDE PRESS
P.O. Box 301
Holicong, PA 18928-0301

www.wildsidepress.com

Table of Contents

How Fear Came

The stream is shrunk — the pool is dry,
And we be comrades, thou and I;
With fevered jowl and dusty flank
Each jostling each along the bank;
And by one drouthy fear made still,
Forgoing thought of quest or kill.
Now 'neath his dam the fawn may see,
The lean Pack-wolf as cowed as he,
And the tall buck, unflinching, note
The fangs that tore his father's throat.
The pools are shrunk — the streams are dry,
And we be playmates, thou and I,
Till yonder cloud — Good Hunting! — loose
The rain that breaks our Water Truce.

*T*he Law of the Jungle — which is by far the oldest law in the world — has arranged for almost every kind of accident that may befall the Jungle People, till now its code is as perfect as time and custom can make it. You will remember that Mowgli spent a great part of his life in the Seeonee Wolf-Pack, learning the Law from Baloo, the Brown Bear; and it was Baloo who told him, when the boy grew impatient at the constant orders, that the Law was like the Giant Creeper, because it dropped across everyone's back and no one could escape. "When thou hast lived as long as I have, Little Brother, thou wilt see how all the Jungle obeys at least one Law. And that will be no pleasant sight," said Baloo.

This talk went in at one ear and out at the other, for a boy who spends his life eating and sleeping does not worry about anything till it actually stares him in the face. But, one year, Baloo's words came true, and Mowgli saw all the Jungle working under the Law.

It began when the winter Rains failed almost entirely, and Ikki, the Porcupine, meeting Mowgli in a bamboo-thicket, told him that the wild yams were drying up. Now everybody knows that Ikki is ridiculously fastidious in his choice of food, and will eat nothing but the very best and ripest. So Mowgli laughed and said, "What is that to me?"

"Not much *now*," said Ikki, rattling his quills in a stiff, uncomfortable way, "but later we shall see. Is there anymore diving into the deep rock-pool below the Bee-Rocks, Little Brother?"

"No. The foolish water is going all away, and I do not wish to break my head," said Mowgii, who, in those days, was quite sure that he knew as much as any five of the Jungle People put together.

"That is thy loss. A small crack might let in some wisdom." Ikki ducked quickly to prevent Mowgli from pulling his nose-bristles, and Mowgli told Baloo what Ikki had said. Baloo looked very grave, and mumbled half to himself: "If I were alone I would change my hunting-grounds now, before the others began to think. And yet — hunting among strangers ends in fighting; and they might hurt the Man-cub. We must wait and see how the mohwa blooms."

That spring the mohwa tree, that Baloo was so fond of, never flowered. The greeny, cream-colored, waxy blossoms were heat-killed before they were born, and only a few bad-smelling petals came down when he stood on his hind legs and shook the tree. Then, inch by inch, the untempered heat crept into the heart of the Jungle, turning it yellow, brown, and at last black. The green growths in the sides of the ravines burned up to broken wires and curled films of dead stuff; the hidden pools sank down and caked over, keeping the last least footmark on their edges as if it had been cast in iron; the juicy-stemmed creepers fell away from the trees they clung to and died at their feet; the bamboos withered, clanking when the hot winds blew, and the moss peeled off the rocks deep in the Jungle, till they were as bare and as hot as the quivering blue boulders in the bed of the stream.

The birds and the monkey-people went north early in the year, for they knew what was coming; and the deer and the wild pig broke far away to the perished fields of the villages, dying sometimes before the eyes of men too weak to kill them. Chil, the Kite, stayed and grew fat, for there was a great deal of carrion, and evening after evening he brought the news to the beasts, too weak to force their way to fresh hunting-grounds, that the sun was killing the Jungle for three days' flight in every direction.

Mowgli, who had never known what real hunger meant, fell back on stale honey, three years old, scraped out of deserted rock-hives — honey black as a sloe, and dusty with dried sugar. He hunted, too, for deep-boring grubs under the bark of the trees, and robbed the wasps of their new broods. All the game in the jungle was no more than skin and bone, and Bagheera could kill thrice in a night, and hardly get a full meal. But the want of water was the worst, for though the Jungle

People drink seldom they must drink deep.

And the heat went on and on, and sucked up all the moisture, till at last the main channel of the Waingunga was the only stream that carried a trickle of water between its dead banks; and when Hathi, the wild elephant, who lives for a hundred years and more, saw a long, lean blue ridge of rock show dry in the very center of the stream, he knew that he was looking at the Peace Rock, and then and there he lifted up his trunk and proclaimed the Water Truce, as his father before him had proclaimed it fifty years ago. The deer, wild pig, and buffalo took up the cry hoarsely; and Chil, the Kite, flew in great circles far and wide, whistling and shrieking the warning.

By the Law of the Jungle it is death to kill at the drinking-places when once the Water Truce has been declared. The reason of this is that drinking comes before eating. Everyone in the Jungle can scramble along somehow when only game is scarce; but water is water, and when there is but one source of supply, all hunting stops while the Jungle People go there for their needs. In good seasons, when water was plentiful, those who came down to drink at the Waingunga — or anywhere else, for that matter — did so at the risk of their lives, and that risk made no small part of the fascination of the night's doings. To move down so cunningly that never a leaf stirred; to wade knee-deep in the roaring shallows that drown all noise from behind; to drink, looking backward over one shoulder, every muscle ready for the first desperate bound of keen terror; to roll on the sandy margin, and return, wet-muzzled and well plumped out, to the admiring herd, was a thing that all tall-antlered young bucks took a delight in, precisely because they knew that at any moment Bagheera or Shere Khan might leap upon them and bear them down. But now all that life-and-death fun was ended, and the Jungle People came up, starved and weary, to the shrunken river, — tiger, bear, deer, buffalo, and pig, all together, — drank the fouled waters, and hung above them, too exhausted to move off.

The deer and the pig had tramped all day in search of something better than dried bark and withered leaves. The buffaloes had found no wallows to be cool in, and no green crops to steal. The snakes had left the Jungle and come down to the river in the hope of finding a stray frog. They curled round wet stones, and never offered to strike when the nose of a rooting pig dislodged them. The river-turtles had long ago been killed by Bagheera, cleverest of hunters, and the fish had buried themselves deep in the dry mud. Only the Peace Rock lay across the shallows like a long snake, and the little tired ripples hissed as they dried on its hot side.

It was here that Mowgli came nightly for the cool and the companionship. The most hungry of his enemies would hardly have cared for the boy then, His naked hide made him seem more lean and wretched than any of his fellows. His hair was bleached to tow color by the sun; his ribs stood out like the ribs of a basket, and the lumps on his knees and elbows, where he was used to track on all fours, gave his shrunken limbs the look of knotted grass-stems. But his eye, under his matted forelock, was cool and quiet, for Bagheera was his adviser in this time of trouble, and told him to go quietly, hunt slowly, and never, on any account, to lose his temper.

"It is an evil time," said the Black Panther, one furnace-hot evening, "but it will go if we can live till the end. Is thy stomach full, Man-cub?"

"There is stuff in my stomach, but I get no good of it. Think you, Bagheera, the Rains have forgotten us and will never come again?"

"Not I! We shall see the mohwa in blossom yet, and the little fawns all fat with new grass. Come down to the Peace Rock and hear the news. On my back, Little Brother."

"This is no time to carry weight. I can still stand alone, but — indeed we be no fatted bullocks, we two."

Bagheera looked along his ragged, dusty flank and whispered. "Last night I killed a bullock under the yoke. So low was I brought that I think I should not have dared to spring if he had been loose. *Wou!*"

Mowgli laughed. "Yes, we be great hunters now," said he. "I am very bold — to eat grubs," and the two came down together through the crackling undergrowth to the river-bank and the lace-work of shoals that ran out from it in every direction.

"The water cannot live long," said Baloo, joining them. "Look across. Yonder are trails like the roads of Man."

On the level plain of the farther bank the stiff jungle-grass had died standing, and, dying, had mummied. The beaten tracks of the deer and the pig, all heading toward the river, had striped that colorless plain with dusty gullies driven through the ten-foot grass, and, early as it was, each long avenue was full of first-comers hastening to the water. You could hear the does and fawns coughing in the snufflike dust.

Up-stream, at the bend of the sluggish pool round the Peace Rock, and Warden of the Water Truce, stood Hathi, the wild elephant, with his sons, gaunt and gray in the moonlight, rocking to and fro — always rocking. Below him a little were the vanguard of the deer; below these, again, the pig and the wild buffalo; and on the opposite bank, where the tall trees came down to the water's edge, was the place set apart for the Eaters of Flesh — the tiger, the wolves, the panther, the bear, and the others.

"We are under one Law, indeed," said Bagheera, wading into the water and looking across at the lines of clicking horns and starting eyes where the deer and the pig pushed each other to and fro. "Good hunting, all you of my blood," he added, lying own at full length, one flank thrust out of the shallows; and then, between his teeth, "But for that which is the Law it would be *very* good hunting."

The quick-spread ears of the deer caught the last sentence, and a frightened whisper ran along the ranks. "The Truce! Remember the Truce!"

"Peace there, peace!" gurgled Hathi, the wild elephant. "The Truce holds, Bagheera. This is no time to talk of hunting."

"Who should know better than I?" Bagheera answered, rolling his yellow eyes up-stream. "I am an eater of turtles — a fisher of frogs. Ngaayah! Would I could get good from chewing branches!"

"*We* wish so, very greatly," bleated a young fawn, who had only been born that spring, and did not at all like it. Wretched as the Jungle People were, even Hathi could not help chuckling; while Mowgli, lying on his elbows in the warm water, laughed aloud, and beat up the scum with his feet.

"Well spoken, little bud-horn," Bagheera purred. "When the Truce ends that shall be remembered in thy favor," and he looked keenly through the darkness to make sure of recognizing the fawn again.

Gradually the talking spread up and down the drinking-places. One could hear the scuffling, snorting pig asking for more room; the buffaloes grunting among themselves as they lurched out across the sand-bars, and the deer telling pitiful stories of their long footsore wanderings in quest of food. Now and again they asked some question of the Eaters of Flesh across the river, but all the news was bad, and the roaring hot wind of the Jungle came and went between the rocks and the rattling branches, and scattered twigs, and dust on the water.

"The menfolk, too, they die beside their ploughs," said a young sambhur. "I passed three between sunset and night. They lay still, and their Bullocks with them. We also shall lie still in a little."

"The river has fallen since last night," said Baloo. "O Hathi, hast thou ever seen the like of this drought?"

"It will pass, it will pass," said Hathi, squirting water along his back and sides.

"We have one here that cannot endure long," said Baloo; and he looked toward the boy he loved.

"I?" said Mowgli indignantly, sitting up in the water. "I have no long fur to cover my bones, but — but if *thy* hide were taken off, Baloo —"

Hathi shook all over at the idea, and Baloo said severely:

"Man-cub, that is not seemly to tell a Teacher of the Law. Never have I been seen without my hide."

"Nay, I meant no harm, Baloo; but only that thou art, as it were, like the cocoanut in the husk, and I am the same cocoanut all naked. Now that brown husk of thine —" Mowgli was sitting cross-legged, and explaining things with his forefinger in his usual way, when Bagheera put out a paddy paw and pulled him over backward into the water.

"Worse and worse," said the Black Panther, as the boy rose spluttering. "First Baloo is to be skinned, and now he is a cocoanut. Be careful that he does not do what the ripe cocoanuts do."

"And what is that?" said Mowgli, off his guard for the minute, though that is one of the oldest catches in the Jungle.

"Break thy head," said Bagheera quietly, pulling him

under again.

"It is not good to make a jest of thy teacher," said the bear, when Mowgli had been ducked for the third time.

"Not good! What would ye have? That naked thing running to and fro makes a monkey-jest of those who have once been good hunters, and pulls the best of us by the whiskers for sport." This was Shere Khan, the Lame Tiger, limping down to the water. He waited a little to enjoy the sensation he made among the deer on the opposite to lap, growling: "The jungle has become a whelping-ground for naked cubs now. Look at me, Man-cub!"

Mowgli looked — stared, rather — as insolently as he knew how, and in a minute Shere Khan turned away uneasily. "Man-cub this, and Man-cub that," he rumbled, going on with his drink, "the cub is neither man nor cub, or he would have been afraid. Next season I shall have to beg his leave for a drink. Augrh!"

"That may come, too," said Bagheera, looking him steadily between the eyes. "That may come, too — Faugh, Shere Khan! — what new shame hast thou brought here?"

The Lame Tiger had dipped his chin and jowl in the water, and dark, oily streaks were floating from it down-stream.

"Man!" said Shere Khan coolly, "I killed an hour since." He went on purring and growling to himself.

The line of beasts shook and wavered to and fro, and a whisper went up that grew to a cry. "Man! Man! He has killed Man!" Then all looked towards Hathi, the wild elephant, but he seemed not to hear. Hathi never does anything till the time comes, and that is one of the reasons why he lives so long.

"At such a season as this to kill Man! Was no other game afoot?" said Bagheera scornfully, drawing himself out of the tainted water, and shaking each paw, cat-fashion, as he did so.

"I killed for choice — not for food." The horrified whisper began again, and Hathi's watchful little white eye cocked itself in Shere Khan's direction. "For choice," Shere Khan drawled. "Now come I to drink and make me clean again. Is there any to forbid?"

Bagheera's back began to curve like a bamboo in a high wind, but Hathi lifted up his trunk and spoke quietly.

"Thy kill was from choice?" he asked; and when Hathi asks a question it is best to answer.

"Even so. It was my right and my Night. Thou knowest, O Hathi." Shere Khan spoke almost courteously.

"Yes, I know," Hathi answered; and, after a little silence, "Hast thou drunk thy fill?"

"For tonight, yes."

"Go, then. The river is to drink, and not to defile. None but the Lame Tiger would so have boasted of his right at this season when — when we suffer together — Man and Jungle People alike. Clean or unclean, get to thy lair, Shere Khan!"

The last words rang out like silver trumpets, and Hathi's three sons rolled forward half a pace, though there was no need. Shere Khan slunk away, not daring to growl, for he knew — what everyone else knows — that when the last comes to the last, Hathi is the Master of the Jungle.

"What is this right Shere Khan speaks of?" Mowgli whispered in Bagheera's ear. "To kill Man is always, shameful. The Law says so. And yet Hathi says —"

"Ask him. I do not know, Little Brother. Right or no right, if Hathi had not spoken I would have taught that lame butcher his lesson. To come to the Peace Rock fresh from a kill of Man — and to boast of it —

is a jackal's trick. Besides, he tainted the good water."

Mowgli waited for a minute to pick up his courage, because no one cared to address Hathi directly, and then he cried: "What is Shere Khan's right, O Hathi?" Both banks echoed his words, for all the People of the Jungle are intensely curious, and they had just seen something that none except Baloo, who looked very thoughtful, seemed to understand.

"It is an old tale," said Hathi; "a tale older than the Jungle. Keep silence along the banks and I will tell that tale."

There was a minute or two of pushing a shouldering among the pigs and the buffalo, and then the leaders of the herds grunted, one after another, "We wait," and Hathi strode forward, till he was nearly knee-deep in the pool by the Peace Rock. Lean and wrinkled and yellow-tusked though he was, he looked what the Jungle knew him to be — their master.

"Ye know, children," he began, "that of all things ye most fear Man"; and there was a mutter of agreement.

"This tale touches thee, Little Brother," said Bagheera to Mowgli.

"I? I am of the Pack — a hunter of the Free People," Mowgli answered. "What have I to do with Man?"

"And ye do not know why ye fear Man?" Hathi went on. "This is the reason. In the beginning of the Jungle, and none know when that was, we of the Jungle walked together, having no fear of one another. In those days there was no drought, and leaves and flowers and fruit grew on the same tree, and we ate nothing at all except leaves and flowers and grass and fruit and bark."

"I am glad I was not born in those days," said Bagheera. "Bark is only good to sharpen claws."

"And the Lord of the Jungle was Tha, the First of the Elephants. He drew the Jungle out of deep waters with his trunk; and where he made furrows in the ground with his tusks, there the rivers ran; and where he struck with his foot, there rose ponds of good water; and when he blew through his trunk, — thus, — the trees fell. That was the manner in which the Jungle was made by Tha; and so the tale was told to me."

"It has not lost fat in the telling," Bagheera whispered, and Mowgli laughed behind his hand.

"In those days there was no corn or melons or pepper or sugar-cane, nor were there any little huts such as ye have all seen; and the Jungle People knew nothing of Man, but lived in the Jungle together, making one people. But presently they began to dispute over their food, though there was grazing enough for all. They were lazy. Each wished to eat where he lay, as sometimes we can do now when the spring rains are good. Tha, the First of the Elephants, was busy making new jungles and leading the rivers in their beds. He could not walk in all places; therefore he made the First of the Tigers the master and the judge of the Jungle, to whom the Jungle People should bring their disputes. In those days the First of the Tigers ate fruit and grass with the others. He was as large as I am, and he was very beautiful, in color all over like the blossom of the yellow creeper. There was never stripe nor bar upon his hide in those good days when this the Jungle was new. All the Jungle People came before him without fear, and his word was the Law of all the Jungle. We were then, remember ye, one people.

"Yet upon a night there was a dispute between two bucks — a grazing-quarrel such as ye now settle with the horns and the fore-feet — and it is said that as the two spoke together before the First of the First of the Tigers lying among the flowers, a buck pushed him with his horns, and the First of the Tigers forgot that he was the master and judge of the Jungle, and, leaping upon that buck, broke his neck.

"Till that night never one of us had died, and the First of the Tigers, seeing what he had done, and being made foolish by the scent of the blood, ran away into the marshes of the North, and we of the Jungle, left without a judge, fell to fighting among ourselves; and Tha heard the noise of it and came back. Then some of us said this and some of us said that, but he saw the dead buck among the flowers, and asked who had killed, and we of the Jungle would not tell because the smell of the blood made us foolish. We ran to and fro in circles, capering and crying out and shaking our heads. Then Tha gave an order to the trees that hang low, and to the trailing creepers of the Jungle, that they should mark the killer of the buck so that he should know him again, and he said, 'Who will now be master of the Jungle People?' Then up leaped the Gray Ape who lives in the branches, and said, 'I will now be master of the Jungle.'

At this Tha laughed, and said, "So be it," and went away very angry.

"Children, ye know the Gray Ape. He was then as he is now. At the first he made a wise face for himself, but in a little while he began to scratch and to leap up and down, and when Tha came back he found the Gray Ape hanging, head down, from a bough, mocking those who stood below; and they mocked him again. And so there was no Law in the Jungle — only foolish talk and senseless words.

"Then Tha called us all together and said: 'The first of your masters has brought Death into the Jungle, and the second Shame. Now it is time there was a Law, and a Law that ye must not break. Now ye shall know Fear, and when ye have found him ye shall know that he is your master, and the rest shall follow.' Then we of the jungle said, 'What is Fear?' And Tha said, 'Seek till ye find.' So we went up and down the Jungle seeking for

Fear, and presently the buffaloes —"

"Ugh!" said Mysa, the leader of the buffaloes, from their sandbank.

"Yes, Mysa, it was the buffaloes. They came back with the news that in a cave in the Jungle sat Fear, and that he had no hair, and went upon his hind legs. Then we of the Jungle followed the herd till we came to that cave, and Fear stood at the mouth of it, and he was, as the buffaloes had said, hairless, and he walked upon his hinder legs. When he saw us he cried out, and his voice filled us with the fear that we have now of that voice when we hear it, and we ran away, tramping upon and tearing each other because we were afraid. That night, so it was told to me, we of the Jungle did not lie down together as used to be our custom, but each tribe drew off by itself — the pig with the pig, the deer with the deer; horn to horn, hoof to hoof, — like keeping to like, and so lay shaking in the Jungle.

"Only the First of the Tigers was not with us, for he was still hidden in the marshes of the North, and when word was brought to him of the Thing we had seen in the cave, he said. 'I will go to this Thing and break his neck.' So he ran all the night till he came to the cave; but the trees and the creepers on his path, remembering the order that Tha had given, let down their branches and marked him as he ran, drawing their fingers across his back, his flank, his forehead, and his jowl. Wherever they touched him there was a mark and a stripe upon his yellow hide. *And those stripes do this children wear to this day!* When he came to the cave, Fear, the Hairless One, put out his hand and called him 'The Striped One that comes by night,' and the First of the Tigers was afraid of the Hairless One, and ran back to the swamps howling."

Mowgli chuckled quietly here, his chin in the water.

"So loud did he howl that Tha heard him and said,

'What is the sorrow?' And the First of the Tigers, lifting up his muzzle to the new-made sky, which is now so old, said: 'Give me back my power, O Tha. I am made ashamed before all the Jungle, and I have run away from a Hairless One, and he has called me a shameful name.' 'And why?' said Tha. 'Because I am smeared with the mud of the marshes,' said the First of the Tigers. 'Swim, then, and roll on the wet grass, and if it be mud it will wash away,' said Tha; and the First of the Tigers swam, and rolled and rolled upon the grass, till the Jungle ran round and round before his eyes, but not one little bar upon all his hide was changed, and Tha, watching him, laughed. Then the First of the Tigers said: 'What have I done that this comes to me?' Tha said, 'Thou hast killed the buck, and thou hast let Death loose in the Jungle, and with Death has come Fear, so that the people of the Jungle are afraid one of the other, as thou art afraid of the Hairless One.' The First of the Tigers said, 'They will never fear me, for I knew them since the beginning.' Tha said, 'Go and see.' And the First of the Tigers ran to and fro, calling aloud to the deer and the pig and the sambhur and the porcupine and all the Jungle Peoples, and they all ran away from him who had been their judge, because they were afraid.

"Then the First of the Tigers came back, and his pride was broken in him, and, beating his head upon the ground, he tore up the earth with all his feet and said: 'Remember that I was once the Master of the Jungle. Do not forget me, O Tha! Let my children remember that I was once without shame or fear!' And Tha said: 'This much I will do, because thou and I together saw the Jungle made. For one night in each year it shall be as it was before the buck was killed — for thee and for thy children. In that one night, if ye meet the Hairless One — and his name is Man — ye shall not be afraid of him, but he shall he afraid of you, as though ye were judges of the Jungle and masters of all things. Show him mercy in that night of his fear, for thou hast known what Fear is.'

"Then the First of the Tigers answered, 'I am content'; but when next he drank he saw the black stripes upon his flank and his side, and he remembered the name that the Hairless One had given him, and he was angry. For a year he lived in the marshes waiting till Tha should keep his promise. And upon a night when the jackal of the Moon [the Evening Star] stood clear of the Jungle, he felt that his Night was upon him, and he went to that cave to meet the Hairless One. Then it happened as Tha promised, for the Hairless One fell down before him and lay along the ground, and the First of the Tigers struck him and broke his back, for he thought that there was but one such Thing in the Jungle, and that he had killed Fear. Then, nosing above the kill, he heard Tha coming down from the woods of the North, and presently the voice of the First of the Elephants, which is the voice that we hear now —"

The thunder was rolling up and down the dry, scarred hills, but it brought no rain — only heat — lightning that flickered along the ridges — and Hathi went on: "*That* was the voice he heard, and it said: 'Is this thy mercy?' The First of the Tigers licked his lips and said: 'What matter? I have killed Fear.' And Tha said: 'O blind and foolish! Thou hast untied the feet of Death, and he will follow thy trail till thou diest. Thou hast taught Man to kill!'

"The First of the Tigers, standing stiffly to his kill, said. 'He is as the buck was. There is no Fear. Now I will judge the Jungle Peoples once more.'

"And Tha said: 'Never again shall the Jungle Peoples come to thee. They shall never cross thy trail, nor sleep near thee, nor follow after thee, nor browse by thy lair.

Only Fear shall follow thee, and with a blow that thou canst not see he shall bid thee wait his pleasure. He shall make the ground to open under thy feet, and the creeper to twist about thy neck, and the tree-trunks to grow together about thee higher than thou canst leap, and at the last he shall take thy hide to wrap his cubs when they are cold. Thou hast shown him no mercy, and none will he show thee.'

"The First of the Tigers was very bold, for his Night was still on him, and he said: 'The Promise of Tha is the Promise of Tha. He will not take away my Night?' And Tha said: 'The one Night is thine, as I have said, but there is a price to pay. Thou hast taught Man to kill, and he is no slow learner.'

"The First of the Tigers said: 'He is here under my foot, and his back is broken. Let the Jungle know I have killed Fear.'

"Then Tha laughed, and said: 'Thou hast killed one of many, but thou thyself shalt tell the Jungle — for thy Night is ended.'

"So the day came; and from the mouth of the cave went out another Hairless One, and he saw the kill in the path, and the First of the Tigers above it, and he took a pointed stick —"

"They throw a thing that cuts now," said Ikki, rustling down the bank; for Ikki was considered uncommonly good eating by the Gonds — they called him Ho-Igoo — and he knew something of the wicked little Gondee axe that whirls across a clearing like a dragon-fly.

"It was a pointed stick, such as they put in the foot of a pit-trap," said Hathi, "and throwing it, he struck the First of the Tigers deep in the flank. Thus it happened as Tha said, for the First of the Tigers ran howling up and down the Jungle till he tore out the stick, and all the Jungle knew that the Hairless One could strike from far off, and they feared more than before. So it came about that the First of the Tigers taught the Hairless One to kill — and ye know what harm that has since done to all our peoples — through the noose, and the pitfall, and the hidden trap, and the flying stick and the stinging fly that comes out of white smoke [Hathi meant the rifle], and the Red Flower that drives us into the open. Yet for one night in the year the Hairless One fears the Tiger, as Tha promised, and never has the Tiger given him cause to be less afraid. Where he finds him, there he kills him, remembering how the First of the Tigers was made ashamed. For the rest, Fear walks up and down the Jungle by day and by night."

"Ahi! Aoo!" said the deer, thinking of what it all meant to them.

"And only when there is one great Fear over all, as there is now, can we of the Jungle lay aside our little fears, and meet together in one place as we do now."

"For one night only does Man fear the Tiger?" said Mowgli.

"For one night only," said Hathi.

"But I — but we — but all the Jungle knows that Shere Khan kills Man twice and thrice in a moon."

"Even so. *Then* he springs from behind and turns his head aside as he strikes, for he is full of fear. If Man looked at him he would run. But on his one Night he goes openly down to the village. He walks between the houses and thrusts his head into the doorway, and the men fall on their faces, and there he does his kill. One kill in that Night."

"Oh!" said Mowgli to himself, rolling over in the water. "*Now* I see why it was Shere Khan bade me look at him! He got no good of it, for he could not hold his eyes steady, and — and I certainly did not fall down at his feet. But then I am not a man, being of the Free

People."

"Umm!" said Bagheera deep in his furry throat. "Does the Tiger know his Night?"

"Never till the Jackal of the Moon stands clear of the evening mist. Sometimes it falls in the dry summer and sometimes in the wet rains — this one Night of the Tiger. But for the First of the Tigers, this would never have been, nor would any of us have known fear."

The deer grunted sorrowfully and Bagheera's lips curled in a wicked smile. "Do men know this — tale?" said he.

"None know it except the tigers, and we, the elephants — the children of Tha. Now ye by the pools have heard it, and I have spoken."

Hathi dipped his trunk into the water as a sign that he did not wish to talk.

"But — but — but," said Mowgli, turning to Baloo, "why did not the First of the Tigers continue to eat grass and leaves and trees? He did but break the buck's neck. He did not *eat*. What led him to the hot meat?"

"The trees and the creepers marked him, Little Brother, and made him the striped thing that we see. Never again would he eat their fruit; but from that day he revenged himself upon the deer, and the others, the Eaters of Grass," said Baloo.

"Then *thou* knowest the tale. Heh? Why have I never heard?"

"Because the Jungle is full of such tales. If I made a beginning there would never be an end to them. Let go my ear, Little Brother."

The Law of the Jungle

*J*ust to give you an idea of the immense variety of the Jungle Law, I have translated into verse (Baloo always recited them in a sort of sing-song) a few of the laws that apply to the wolves. There are, of course, hundreds and hundreds more, but these will do for specimens of the simpler rulings.

Now this is the Law of the Jungle — as old and as
        true as the sky;
And the Wolf that shall keep it may prosper, but the
        Wolf that shall break it must die.

As the creeper that girdles the tree-trunk the Law
        runneth forward and back —
For the strength of the Pack is the Wolf, and the
        strength of the Wolf is the Pack.

Wash daily from nose-tip to tail-tip; drink deeply,
        but never too deep;
And remember the night is for hunting, and forget
        not the day is for sleep.

The jackal may follow the Tiger, but, Cub, when thy
    whiskers are grown,
Remember the Wolf is a hunter — go forth and get
    food of thine own.

Keep peace with the Lords of the Jungle — the Tiger,
    the Panther, the Bear;
And trouble not Hathi the Silent, and mock not the
    Boar in his lair.

When Pack meets with Pack in the Jungle, and
    neither will go from the trail,
Lie down till the leaders have spoken — it may be
    fair words shall prevail.

When ye fight with a Wolf of the Pack, ye must
    fight him alone and afar,
Lest others take part in the quarrel, and the Pack be
    diminished by war.

The Lair of the Wolf is his refuge, and where he has
    made him his home,
Not even the Head Wolf may enter, not even the
    Council may come.

The Lair of the Wolf is his refuge, but where he has
    digged it too plain,
The Council shall send him a message, and so he
    shall change it again.

If ye kill before midnight, be silent, and wake not
    the woods with your bay,
Lest ye frighten the deer from the crops, and the
    brothers go empty away.

Ye may kill for yourselves, and your mates, and your

cubs as they need, and ye can;
But kill not for pleasure of killing, and *seven times
never kill man.*

If ye plunder his Kill from a weaker, devour not all
in thy pride;
Pack-Right is the right of the meanest; so leave him
the head and the hide.

The Kill of the Pack is the meat of the Pack. Ye
must eat where it lies;
And no one may carry away of that meat to his lair,
or he dies.

The Kill of the Wolf is the meat of the Wolf. He
may do what he will,
But, till he has given permission, the Pack may not
eat of that Kill.

Cub-Right is the right of the Yearling. From all of
his Pack he may claim
Full-gorge when the killer has eaten; and none may
refuse him the same.

Lair-Right is the right of the Mother. From all of
her year she may claim
One haunch of each kill for her litter, and none
may deny her the same.

Cave-Right is the right of the Father — to hunt by
himself for his own.
He is freed of all calls to the Pack; he is judged by
the Council alone.

Because of his age and his cunning, because of his
gripe and his paw,

In all that the Law leaveth open, the word of the
    Head Wolf is Law.

Now these are the Laws of the Jungle, and many and
    mighty are they;
But the head and the hoof of the Law and the
    haunch and the hump is — Obey!

The Miracle of Purun Bhagat

The night we felt the earth would move
   We stole and plucked him by the hand,
Because we loved him with the love
   That knows but cannot understand.

And when the roaring hillside broke,
   And all our world fell down in rain,
We saved him, we the Little Folk;
   But lo! he does not come again!

Mourn now, we saved him for the sake
   Of such poor love as wild ones may.
Mourn ye! Our brother will not wake,
   And his own kind drive us away!
             Dirge of the Langurs

*T*here was once a man in India who was Prime Minister of one of the semi-independent native States in the northwestern part of the country. He was a

Brahmin, so high-caste that caste ceased to have any particular meaning for him; and his father had been an important official in the gay-colored tag-rag and bobtail of an old-fashioned Hindu Court. But as Purun Dass grew up he felt that the old order of things was changing, and that if anyone wished to get on in the world he must stand well with the English, and imitate all that the English believed to be good. At the same time a native official must keep his own master's favor. This was a difficult game, but the quiet, close-mouthed young Brahmin, helped by a good English education at a Bombay University, played it coolly, and rose, step by step, to be Prime Minister of the kingdom. That is to say, he held more real power than his master the Maharajah.

When the old king — who was suspicious of the English, their railways and telegraphs — died, Purun Dass stood high with his young successor, who had been tutored by an Englishman; and between them, though he always took care that his master should have the credit, they established schools for little girls, made roads, and started State dispensaries and shows of agricultural implements, and published a yearly blue-book on the "Moral and Material Progress of the State," and the Foreign Office and the Government of India were delighted. Very few native States take up English progress altogether, for they will not believe, as Purun Dass showed he did, that what was good for the Englishman must be twice as good for the Asiatic. The Prime Minister became the honored friend of Viceroys, and Governors, and Lieutenant-Governors, and medical missionaries, and common missionaries, and hard-riding English officers who came to shoot in the State preserves, as well as of whole hosts of tourists who traveled up and down India in the cold weather, showing how things ought to be managed. In his spare time he would endow scholarships for the study of medicine and manufactures on strictly English lines, and write letters to the "Pioneer," the greatest Indian daily paper, explaining his master's aims and objects.

At last he went to England on a visit, and had to pay enormous sums to the priests when he came back; for even so high-caste a Brahmin as Purun Dass lost caste by crossing the black sea. In London he met and talked with everyone worth knowing — men whose names go all over the world — and saw a great deal more than he said. He was given honorary degrees by learned universities, and he made speeches and talked of Hindu social reform to English ladies in evening dress, till all London cried, "This is the most fascinating man we have ever met at dinner since cloths were first laid."

When he returned to India there was a blaze of glory, for the Viceroy himself made a special visit to confer upon the Maharajah the Grand Cross of the Star of India — all diamonds and ribbons and enamel; and at the same ceremony, while the cannon boomed, Purun Dass was made a Knight Commander of the Order of the Indian Empire; so that his name stood Sir Purun Dass, K.C.I.E.

That evening, at dinner in the big Viceregal tent, he stood up with the badge and the collar of the Order on his breast, and replying to the toast of his master's health, made a speech few Englishmen could have bettered.

Next month, when the city had returned to its sunbaked quiet, he did a thing no Englishman would have dreamed of doing; for, so far as the world's affairs went, he died. The jeweled order of his knighthood went back to the Indian Government, and a new Prime Minister was appointed to the charge of affairs, and a great game of General Post began in all the subordinate appointments. The priests knew what had happened, and the people guessed; but India is the one place in the world where a man can do as he pleases and nobody asks why; and the fact that Dewan Sir Purun Dass, K.C.I.E., had resigned position, palace, and power, and taken up the begging-bowl and ochre-colored dress of a Sunnyasi, or holy man, was considered nothing extraordinary. He had been, as the Old Law recommends, twenty years a youth, twenty years a fighter, — though he had never carried a weapon in his life, — and twenty years head of a household. He had used his wealth and his power for what he knew both to be worth; he had taken honor when it came his way; he had seen men and cities far and near, and men and cities had stood up and honored him. Now he would let those things go, as a man drops the cloak he no longer needs.

Behind him, as he walked through the city gates, an antelope skin and brass-handled crutch under his arm, and a begging-bowl of polished brown coco-de-mer in his hand, barefoot, alone, with eyes cast on the ground — behind him they were firing salutes from the bastions in honor of his happy successor. Purun Dass nodded. All that life was ended; and he bore it no more ill-will or good-will than a man bears to a colorless dream of the night. He was a Sunnyasi — a houseless, wandering mendicant, depending on his neighbors for his daily bread; and so long as there is a morsel to divide in India, neither priest nor beggar starves. He had never in his life tasted meat, and very seldom eaten even fish. A five-pound note would have covered his personal expenses for food through any one of the many years in which he had been absolute master of millions of money. Even when he was being lionised in London he had held before him his dream of peace and quiet — the long, white, dusty Indian road, printed all over with bare feet, the incessant, slow-moving traffic, and the sharp-smelling wood smoke curling up under the fig trees in the twilight, where the wayfarers sit at their evening meal.

When the time came to make that dream true the Prime Minister took the proper steps, and in three days you might more easily have found a bubble in the trough of the long Atlantic seas, than Purun Dass among the roving, gathering, separating millions of India.

At night his antelope skin was spread where the darkness overtook him — sometimes in a Sunnyasi monastery by the roadside; sometimes by a mud-pillar shrine of Kala Pir, where the Jogis, who are another misty division of holy men, would receive him as they do those who know what castes and divisions are worth; sometimes on the outskirts of a little Hindu village, where the children would steal up with the food their parents had prepared; and sometimes on the pitch of the bare grazing-grounds, where the flame of his stick fire waked the drowsy camels. It was all one to Purun Dass — or Purun Bhagat, as he called himself now. Earth, people, and food were all one. But unconsciously his feet drew him away northward and eastward; from the south to Rohtak; from Rohtak to Kurnool; from Kurnool to ruined Samanah, and then up-stream along the dried bed of the Gugger river that fills only when the rain falls in the hills, till one day he saw the far line of the great Himalayas.

Then Purun Bhagat smiled, for he remembered that his mother was of Rajput Brahmin birth, from Kulu way — a Hill-woman, always home-sick for the snows — and that the least touch of Hill blood draws a man in the end back to where he belongs.

"Yonder," said Purun Bhagat, breasting the lower slopes of the Sewaliks, where the cacti stand up like seven-branched candlesticks — "yonder I shall sit down and get knowledge"; and the cool wind of the Himalayas whistled about his ears as he trod the road that led to Simla.

The last time he had come that way it had been in state, with a clattering cavalry escort, to visit the gentlest and most affable of Viceroys; and the two had talked for an hour together about mutual friends in London, and what the Indian common folk really thought of things. This time Purun Bhagat paid no calls, but leaned on the rail of the Mall, watching that glorious view of the Plains spread out forty miles below, till a native Mohammedan policeman told him he was obstructing traffic; and Purun Bhagat salaamed reverently to the Law, because he knew the value of it, and was seeking for a Law of his own. Then he moved on, and slept that night in an empty hut at Chota Simla, which looks like the very last end of the earth, but it was only the beginning of his journey. He followed the Himalaya-Tibet road, the little ten-foot track that is blasted out of solid rock, or strutted out on timbers over gulfs a thousand feet deep; that dips into warm, wet, shut-in valleys, and climbs out across bare, grassy hill-shoulders where the sun strikes like a burning-glass; or turns through dripping, dark forests where the tree-ferns dress the trunks from head to heel, and the pheasant calls to his mate. And he met Tibetan herdsmen with their dogs and flocks of sheep, each sheep with a little bag of borax on his back, and wandering wood-cutters, and cloaked and blanketed Lamas from Tibet, coming into India on pilgrimage, and envoys of little solitary Hill-states, posting furiously on ring-streaked and piebald ponies, or the cavalcade of a Rajah paying a visit; or else for a long, clear day he would see nothing more than a black bear grunting and rooting below in the valley. When he first started, the roar of the world he had left still rang in his ears, as the roar of a tunnel rings long after the train has passed through; but when he had put the Mutteeanee Pass behind him that was all done, and Purun Bhagat was alone with himself, walking, wondering, and thinking, his eyes on the ground, and his thoughts with the clouds.

One evening he crossed the highest pass he had met till then — it had been a two-day's climb — and came out on a line of snow-peaks that banded all the horizon — mountains from fifteen to twenty thousand feet high, looking almost near enough to hit with a stone, though they were fifty or sixty miles away. The pass was crowned with dense, dark forest — deodar, walnut, wild cherry, wild olive, and wild pear, but mostly deodar, which is the Himalayan cedar; and under the shadow of the deodars stood a deserted shrine to Kali — who is Durga, who is Sitala, who is sometimes worshipped against the smallpox.

Purun Dass swept the stone floor clean, smiled at the grinning statue, made himself a little mud fireplace at the back of the shrine, spread his antelope skin on a bed of fresh pine-needles, tucked his bairagi — his brass-handled crutch — under his armpit, and sat down to rest.

Immediately below him the hillside fell away, clean and cleared for fifteen hundred feet, where a little village of stone-walled houses, with roofs of beaten earth, clung to the steep tilt. All round it the tiny terraced fields lay out like aprons of patchwork on the knees of the mountain, and cows no bigger than beetles grazed between the smooth stone circles of the threshing-floors. Looking across the valley, the eye was deceived by the size of things, and could not at first realize that what seemed to be low scrub, on the opposite mountain-flank, was in truth a forest of hundred-foot pines. Purun Bhagat saw an eagle swoop across the gigantic hollow, but the great bird dwindled to a dot ere it was half-way over. A few bands of scattered clouds strung up and down the valley, catching on a shoulder of the hills, or rising up and dying out when they were level with the head of the pass. And "Here shall I find peace," said Purun Bhagat.

Now, a Hill-man makes nothing of a few hundred feet up or down, and as soon as the villagers saw the smoke in the deserted shrine, the village priest climbed up the terraced hillside to welcome the stranger.

When he met Purun Bhagat's eyes — the eyes of a man used to control thousands — he bowed to the earth, took the begging-bowl without a word, and returned to the village, saying, "We have at last a holy man. Never have I seen such a man. He is of the Plains — but pale-colored — a Brahmin of the Brahmins." Then all the housewives of the village said, "Think you he will stay with us?" and each did her best to cook the most savory meal for the Bhagat. Hill-food is very simple, but with buckwheat and Indian corn, and rice and red pepper, and little fish out of the stream in the valley, and honey from the fluelike hives built in the stone walls, and dried apricots, and turmeric, and wild ginger, and bannocks of flour, a devout woman can make good things, and it was a full bowl that the priest carried to the Bhagat. Was he going to stay? asked the priest. Would he need a chela — a disciple — to beg for him? Had he a blanket against the cold weather? Was the food good?

Purun Bhagat ate, and thanked the giver. It was in his mind to stay. That was sufficient, said the priest. Let the begging-bowl be placed outside the shrine, in the hollow made by those two twisted roots, and daily should the Bhagat be fed; for the village felt honored that such a man — he looked timidly into the Bhagat's face — should tarry among them.

That day saw the end of Purun Bhagat's wanderings.

He had come to the place appointed for him — the silence and the space. After this, time stopped, and he, sitting at the mouth of the shrine, could not tell whether he were alive or dead; a man with control of his limbs, or a part of the hills, and the clouds, and the shifting rain and sunlight. He would repeat a Name softly to himself a hundred hundred times, till, at each repetition, he seemed to move more and more out of his body, sweeping up to the doors of some tremendous discovery; but, just as the door was opening, his body would drag him back, and, with grief, he felt he was locked up again in the flesh and bones of Purun Bhagat.

Every morning the filled begging-bowl was laid silently in the crutch of the roots outside the shrine. Sometimes the priest brought it; sometimes a Ladakhi trader, lodging in the village, and anxious to get merit, trudged up the path; but, more often, it was the woman who had cooked the meal overnight; and she would murmur, hardly above her breath. "Speak for me before the gods, Bhagat. Speak for such a one, the wife of so-and-so!" Now and then some bold child would be allowed the honor, and Purun Bhagat would hear him drop the bowl and run as fast as his little legs could carry him, but the Bhagat never came down to the village. It was laid out like a map at his feet. He could see the evening gatherings, held on the circle of the threshing-floors, because that was the only level ground; could see the wonderful unnamed green of the young rice, the indigo blues of the Indian corn, the docklike patches of buckwheat, and, in its season, the red bloom of the amaranth, whose tiny seeds, being neither grain nor pulse, make a food that can be lawfully eaten by Hindus in time of fasts.

When the year turned, the roofs of the huts were all little squares of purest gold, for it was on the roofs that they laid out their cobs of the corn to dry. Hiving and harvest, rice-sowing and husking, passed before his eyes, all embroidered down there on the many-sided plots of fields, and he thought of them all, and wondered what they all led to at the long last.

Even in populated India a man cannot a day sit still before the wild things run over him as though he were a rock; and in that wilderness very soon the wild things, who knew Kali's Shrine well, came back to look at the intruder. The langurs, the big gray-whiskered monkeys of the Himalayas, were, naturally, the first, for they are alive with curiosity; and when they had upset the begging-bowl, and rolled it round the floor, and tried their teeth on the brass-handled crutch, and made faces at the antelope skin, they decided that the human being who sat so still was harmless. At evening, they would leap down from the pines, and beg with their hands for things to eat, and then swing off in graceful curves. They liked the warmth of the fire, too, and huddled round it till Purun Bhagat had to push them aside to throw on more fuel; and in the morning, as often as not, he would find a furry ape sharing his blanket. All day long, one or other of the tribe would sit by his side, staring out at the snows, crooning and looking unspeakably wise and sorrowful.

After the monkeys came the barasingh, that big deer which is like our red deer, but stronger. He wished to rub off the velvet of his horns against the cold stones of Kali's statue, and stamped his feet when he saw the man at the shrine. But Purun Bhagat never moved, and, little by little, the royal stag edged up and nuzzled his shoulder. Purun Bhagat slid one cool hand along the hot antlers, and the touch soothed the fretted beast, who bowed his head, and Purun Bhagat very softly rubbed and ravelled off the velvet. Afterward, the barasingh brought his doe and fawn — gentle things that mumbled on the holy man's blanket — or would come alone at night, his eyes green in the fire-flicker, to take his share of fresh walnuts. At last, the musk-deer, the shyest and almost the smallest of the deerlets, came, too, her big rabbity ears erect; even brindled, silent mushick-nabha must needs find out what the light in the shrine meant, and drop out her mooselike nose into Purun Bhagat's lap, coming and going with the shadows of the fire. Purun Bhagat called them all "my brothers," and his low call of "Bhai! Bhai!" would draw them from the forest at noon if they were within ear shot. The Himalayan black bear, moody and suspicious — Sona, who has the V-shaped white mark under his chin — passed that way more than once; and since the Bhagat showed no fear, Sona showed no anger, but watched him, and came closer, and begged a share of the caresses, and a dole of bread or wild berries. Often, in the still dawns, when the Bhagat would climb to the very crest of the pass to watch the red day walking along the peaks of the snows, he would find Sona shuffling and grunting at his heels, thrusting, a curious fore-paw under fallen trunks, and bringing it away with a *whoof* of impatience; or his early steps would wake Sona where he lay curled up, and the great brute, rising erect, would think to fight, till he heard the Bhagat's voice and knew his best friend.

Nearly all hermits and holy men who live apart from the big cities have the reputation of being able to work miracles with the wild things, but all the miracle lies in keeping still, in never making a hasty movement, and, for a long time, at least, in never looking directly at a visitor. The villagers saw the outline of the barasingh stalking like a shadow through the dark forest behind the shrine; saw the minaul, the Himalayan pheasant, blazing in her best colors before Kali's statue; and the langurs on their haunches, inside, playing with the walnut shells. Some of the children, too, had heard Sona singing to himself, bear-fashion, behind the fallen rocks, and the Bhagat's reputation as miracle-worker stood firm.

Yet nothing was farther from his mind than miracles. He believed that all things were one big Miracle, and when a man knows that much he knows something to go upon. He knew for a certainty that there was nothing great and nothing little in this world: and day and night he strove to think out his way into the heart of things, back to the place whence his soul had come.

So thinking, his untrimmed hair fell down about his shoulders, the stone slab at the side of the antelope skin was dented into a little hole by the foot of his brass-handled crutch, and the place between the tree-trunks, where the begging-bowl rested day after day, sunk and wore into a hollow almost as smooth as the brown shell itself; and each beast knew his exact place at the fire. The fields changed their colors with the seasons; the threshing-floors filled and emptied, and filled again and again; and again and again, when winter came, the langurs frisked among the branches feathered with light snow, till the mother-monkeys brought their sad-eyed little babies up from the warmer valleys with the spring. There were few changes in the village. The priest was older, and many of the little children who used to come with the begging-dish sent their own children now; and when you asked of the villagers how long their holy man had lived in Kali's Shrine at the head of the pass, they answered, "Always."

Then came such summer rains as had not been known in the Hills for many seasons. Through three good months the valley was wrapped in cloud and soaking mist — steady, unrelenting downfall, breaking off into thunder-shower after thunder-shower. Kali's Shrine stood above the clouds, for the most part, and there was a whole month in which the Bhagat never caught a glimpse of his village. It was packed away under a white floor of cloud that swayed and shifted and rolled on itself and bulged upward, but never broke from its piers — the streaming flanks of the valley.

All that time he heard nothing but the sound of a million little waters, overhead from the trees, and underfoot along the ground, soaking through the pine-needles, dripping from the tongues of draggled fern, and spouting in newly-torn muddy channels down the slopes. Then the sun came out, and drew forth the good incense of the deodars and the rhododendrons, and that far-off, clean smell which the Hill people call "the smell of the snows." The hot sunshine lasted for a week, and then the rains gathered together for their last downpour, and the water fell in sheets that flayed off the skin of the ground and leaped back in mud. Purun Bhagat heaped his fire high that night, for he was sure his brothers would need warmth; but never a beast came to the shrine, though he called and called till he dropped asleep, wondering what had happened in the woods.

It was in the black heart of the night, the rain drumming like a thousand drums, that he was roused by a plucking at his blanket, and, stretching out, felt the little hand of a langur. "It is better here than in the trees," he said sleepily, loosening a fold of blanket; "take it and be warm." The monkey caught his hand and pulled hard. "Is it food, then?" said Purun Bhagat. "Wait awhile, and I will prepare some." As he kneeled to throw fuel on the fire the langur ran to the door of the shrine, crooned and ran back again, plucking at the man's knee.

"What is it? What is thy trouble, Brother?" said Purun Bhagat, for the langur's eyes were full of things that he could not tell. "Unless one of thy caste be in a trap — and none set traps here — I will not go into that weather. Look, Brother, even the barasingh comes for shelter!"

The deer's antlers clashed as he strode into the shrine, clashed against the grinning statue of Kali. He lowered them in Purun Bhagat's direction and stamped uneasily, hissing through his half-shut nostrils.

"Hai! Hai! Hai!" said the Bhagat, snapping his fingers, "Is *this* payment for a night's lodging?" But the deer pushed him toward the door, and as he did so Purun Bhagat heard the sound of something opening with a sigh, and saw two slabs of the floor draw away from each other, while the sticky earth below smacked its lips.

"Now I see," said Purun Bhagat. "No blame to my brothers that they did not sit by the fire tonight. The mountain is falling. And yet — why should I go?" His eye fell on the empty begging-bowl, and his face changed. "They have given me good food daily since — since I came, and, if I am not swift, tomorrow there will not be one mouth in the valley. Indeed, I must go and warn them below. Back there, Brother! Let me get to the fire."

The barasingh backed unwillingly as Purun Bhagat drove a pine torch deep into the flame, twirling it till it was well lit. "Ah! ye came to warn me," he said, rising. "Better than that we shall do; better than that. Out, now, and lend me thy neck, Brother, for I have but two feet."

He clutched the bristling withers of the barasingh with his right hand, held the torch away with his left, and stepped out of the shrine into the desperate night. There was no breath of wind, but the rain nearly drowned the flare as the great deer hurried down the slope, sliding on his haunches. As soon as they were clear of the forest more of the Bhagat's brothers joined them. He heard, though he could not see, the langurs pressing about him, and behind them the uhh! uhh! of Sona. The rain matted his long white hair into ropes; the water splashed beneath his bare feet, and his yellow robe clung to his frail old body, but he stepped down steadily, leaning against the barasingh. He was no longer a holy man, but Sir Purun Dass, K.C.I.E., Prime Minister of no small State, a man accustomed to command, going out to save life. Down the steep, plashy path they poured all together, the Bhagat and his brothers, down and down till the deer's feet clicked and stumbled on the wall of a threshing-floor, and he snorted because he smelt Man. Now they were at the head of the one crooked village street, and the Bhagat beat with his crutch on the barred windows of the blacksmith's house, as his torch blazed up in the shelter of the eaves. "Up and out!" cried Purun Bhagat; and he did not know his own voice, for it was years since he had spoken aloud to a man. "The hill falls! The hill is falling! Up and out, oh, you within!"

"It is our Bhagat," said the blacksmith's wife. "He stands among his beasts. Gather the little ones and give the call."

It ran from house to house, while the beasts, cramped in the narrow way, surged and huddled round the Bhagat, and Sona puffed impatiently.

The people hurried into the street — they were no more than seventy souls all told — and in the glare of the torches they saw their Bhagat holding back the terrified barasingh, while the monkeys plucked piteously at his skirts, and Sona sat on his haunches and roared.

"Across the valley and up the next hill!" shouted Purun Bhagat. "Leave none behind! We follow!"

Then the people ran as only Hill folk can run, for

they knew that in a landslip you must climb for the highest ground across the valley. They fled, splashing through the little river at the bottom, and panted up the terraced fields on the far side, while the Bhagat and his brethren followed. Up and up the opposite mountain they climbed, calling to each other by name — the roll-call of the village — and at their heels toiled the big barasingh, weighted by the failing strength of Purun Bhagat. At last the deer stopped in the shadow of a deep pinewood, five hundred feet up the hillside. His instinct, that had warned him of the coming slide, told him he would he safe here.

Purun Bhagat dropped fainting by his side, for the chill of the rain and that fierce climb were killing him; but first he called to the scattered torches ahead, "Stay and count your numbers"; then, whispering to the deer as he saw the lights gather in a cluster: "Stay with me, Brother. Stay — till — I — go!"

There was a sigh in the air that grew to a mutter, and a mutter that grew to a roar, and a roar that passed all sense of hearing, and the hillside on which the villagers stood was hit in the darkness, and rocked to the blow. Then a note as steady, deep, and true as the deep C of the organ drowned everything for perhaps five minutes, while the very roots of the pines quivered to it. It died away, and the sound of the rain falling on miles of hard ground and grass changed to the muffled drum of water on soft earth. That told its own tale.

Never a villager — not even the priest — was bold enough to speak to the Bhagat who had saved their lives. They crouched under the pines and waited till the day. When it came they looked across the valley and saw that what had been forest, and terraced field, and track-threaded grazing-ground was one raw, red, fan-shaped smear, with a few trees flung head-down on the scarp. That red ran high up the hill of their refuge, damming back the little river, which had begun to spread into a brick-colored lake. Of the village, of the road to the shrine, of the shrine itself, and the forest behind, there was no trace. For one mile in width and two thousand feet in sheer depth the mountainside had come away bodily, planed clean from head to heel.

And the villagers, one by one, crept through the wood to pray before their Bhagat. They saw the barasingh standing over him, who fled when they came near, and they heard the langurs wailing in the branches, and Sona moaning up the hill; but their Bhagat was dead, sitting cross-legged, his back against a tree, his crutch under his armpit, and his face turned to the northeast.

The priest said: "Behold a miracle after a miracle, for in this very attitude must all Sunnyasis be buried! Therefore where he now is we will build the temple to our holy man."

They built the temple before a year was ended — a little stone-and-earth shrine — and they called the hill the Bhagat's hill, and they worship there with lights and flowers and offerings to this day. But they do not know that the saint of their worship is the late Sir Purun Dass, K.C.I.E., D.C.L., Ph.D., etc., once Prime Minister of the progressive and enlightened State of Mohiniwala, and honorary or corresponding member of more learned and scientific societies than will ever do any good in this world or the next.

A Song of Kabir

Oh, light was the world that he weighed in his
    hands!
Oh, heavy the tale of his fiefs and his lands!
He has gone from the guddee and put on the
    shroud,
And departed in guise of bairagi avowed!

Now the white road to Delhi is mat for his feet,
The sal and the kikar must guard him from heat;
His home is the camp, and the waste, and the
    crowd —
He is seeking the Way as bairagi avowed!

He has looked upon Man, and his eyeballs are clear
(There was One; there is One, and but One, saith
    Kabir);
The Red Mist of Doing has thinned to a cloud —
He has taken the Path for bairagi avowed!

To learn and discern of his brother the clod,
Of his brother the brute, and his brother the God.
He has gone from the council and put on the
    shroud
("Can ye hear?" saith Kabir), a bairagi avowed!

Letting in the Jungle

Veil them, cover them, wall them round —
  Blossom, and creeper, and weed —
Let us forget the sight and the sound,
  The smell and the touch of the breed!

Fat black ash by the altar-stone,
  Here is the white-foot rain,
And the does bring forth in the fields unsown,
  And none shall affright them again;
And the blind walls crumble, unknown, o'erthrown
  And none shall inhabit again!

You will remember that after Mowgli had pinned Shere Khan's hide to the Council Rock, he told as many as were left of the Seeonee Pack that henceforward he would hunt in the Jungle alone; and the four children of Mother and Father Wolf said that they would hunt with him. But it is not easy to change one's life all in a minute — particularly in the Jungle. The first thing Mowgli did, when the disorderly Pack had slunk off, was to go to the home-cave, and sleep for a day and a night. Then he told Mother Wolf and Father

Wolf as much as they could understand of his adventures among men; and when he made the morning sun flicker up and down the blade of his skinning-knife, — the same he had skinned Shere Khan with, — they said he had learned something. Then Akela and Gray Brother had to explain their share of the great buffalo-drive in the ravine, and Baloo toiled up the hill to hear all about it, and Bagheera scratched himself all over with pure delight at the way in which Mowgli had managed his war.

It was long after sunrise, but no one dreamed of going to sleep, and from time to time, during the talk, Mother Wolf would throw up her head, and sniff a deep snuff of satisfaction as the wind brought her the smell of the tiger-skin on the Council Rock.

"But for Akela and Gray Brother here," Mowgli said, at the end, "I could have done nothing. Oh, mother, mother! if thou hadst seen the black herd-bulls pour down the ravine, or hurry through the gates when the Man-Pack flung stones at me!"

"I am glad I did not see that last," said Mother Wolf stiffly. "It is not *my* custom to suffer my cubs to be driven to and fro like jackals. *I* would have taken a price from the Man-Pack; but I would have spared the woman who gave thee the milk. Yes, I would have spared her alone."

"Peace, peace, Raksha!" said Father Wolf, lazily. "Our Frog has come back again — so wise that his own father must lick his feet; and what is a cut, more or less, on the head? Leave Men alone." Baloo and Bagheera both echoed: "Leave Men alone."

Mowgli, his head on Mother Wolf's side, smiled contentedly, and said that, for his own part, he never wished to see, or hear, or smell Man again.

"But what," said Akela, cocking one ear — "but what if men do not leave thee alone, Little Brother?"

"We be *five*," said Gray Brother, looking round at the company, and snapping his jaws on the last word.

"We also might attend to that hunting," said Bagheera, with a little switch-switch of his tail, looking at Baloo. "But why think of men now, Akela?"

"For this reason," the Lone Wolf answered: "when that yellow chief's hide was hung up on the rock, I went back along our trail to the village, stepping in my tracks, turning aside, and lying down, to make a mixed trail in case one should follow us. But when I had fouled the trail so that I myself hardly knew it again, Mang, the Bat, came hawking between the trees, and hung up above me. Said Mang, 'The village of the Man-Pack, where they cast out the Man-cub, hums like a hornet's nest.'"

"It was a big stone that I threw," chuckled Mowgli, who had often amused himself by throwing ripe paw-paws into a hornet's nest, and racing off to the nearest pool before the hornets caught him.

"I asked of Mang what he had seen. He said that the Red Flower blossomed at the gate of the village, and men sat about it carrying guns. Now *I* know, for I have good cause," — Akela looked down at the old dry scars on his flank and side, — "that men do not carry guns for pleasure. Presently, Little Brother, a man with a gun follows our trail — if, indeed, he be not already on it."

"But why should he? Men have cast me out. What more do they need?" said Mowgli angrily.

"Thou art a man, Little Brother," Akela returned. "It is not for *us*, the Free Hunters, to tell thee what thy brethren do, or why."

He had just time to snatch up his paw as the skinning-knife cut deep into the ground below. Mowgli struck quicker than an average human eye could follow but Akela was a wolf; and even a dog, who is very far removed from the wild wolf, his ancestor, can be waked out of deep sleep by a cart-wheel touching his flank, and can spring away unharmed before that wheel comes on.

"Another time," Mowgli said quietly, returning the knife to its sheath, "speak of the Man-Pack and of Mowgli in *two* breaths — not one."

"Phff! That is a sharp tooth," said Akela, snuffing at the blade's cut in the earth, "but living with the Man-Pack has spoiled thine eye, Little Brother. I could have killed a buck while thou wast striking."

Bagheera sprang to his feet, thrust up his head as far as he could, sniffed, and stiffened through every curve in his body. Gray Brother followed his example quickly, keeping a little to his left to get the wind that was blowing from the right, while Akela bounded fifty yards up wind, and, half-crouching, stiffened too. Mowgli looked on enviously. He could smell things as very few human beings could, but he had never reached the hair-triggerlike sensitiveness of a Jungle nose; and his three months in the smoky village had set him back sadly. However, he dampened his finger, rubbed it on his nose, and stood erect to catch the upper scent, which, though it is the faintest, is the truest.

"Man!" Akela growled, dropping on his haunches.

"Buldeo!" said Mowgli, sitting down. "He follows our trail, and yonder is the sunlight on his gun. Look!"

It was no more than a splash of sunlight, for a fraction of a second, on the brass clamps of the old Tower musket, but nothing in the Jungle winks with just that flash, except when the clouds race over the sky. Then a piece of mica, or a little pool, or even a highly-polished leaf will flash like a heliograph. But that day was cloudless and still.

"I knew men would follow," said Akela triumphantly. "Not for nothing have I led the Pack."

The four cubs said nothing, but ran down hill on

their bellies, melting into the thorn and under-brush as a mole melts into a lawn.

"Where go ye, and without word?" Mowgli called.

"H'sh! We roll his skull here before mid-day!" Gray Brother answered.

"Back! Back and wait! Man does not eat Man!" Mowgli shrieked.

"Who was a wolf but now? Who drove the knife at me for thinking he might be Man?" said Akela, as the four wolves turned back sullenly and dropped to heel.

"Am I to give reason for all I choose to, do?" said Mowgli furiously.

"That is Man! There speaks Man!" Bagheera muttered under his whiskers. "Even so did men talk round the King's cages at Oodeypore. We of the Jungle know that Man is wisest of all. If we trusted our ears we should know that of all things he is most foolish." Raising his voice, he added, "The Man-cub is right in this. Men hunt in packs. To kill one, unless we know what the others will do, is bad hunting. Come, let us see what this Man means toward us."

"We will not come," Gray Brother growled. "Hunt alone, Little Brother. *We* know our own minds. The skull would have been ready to bring by now."

Mowgli had been looking from one to the other of his friends, his chest heaving and his eyes full of tears. He strode forward to the wolves, and, dropping on one knee, said: "Do I not know my mind? Look at me!"

They looked uneasily, and when their eyes wandered, he called them back again and again, till their hair stood up all over their bodies, and they trembled in every limb, while Mowgli stared and stared.

"Now," said he, "of us five, which is leader?"

"Thou art leader, Little Brother," said Gray Brother, and he licked Mowgli's foot.

"Follow, then," said Mowgli, and the four followed

at his heels with their tails between their legs.

"This comes of living with the Man-Pack," said Bagheera, slipping down after them. "There is more in the Jungle now than Jungle Law, Baloo."

The old bear said nothing, but he thought many things.

Mowgli cut across noiselessly through the Jungle, at right angles to Buldeo's path, till, parting the undergrowth, he saw the old man, his musket on his shoulder, running up the trail of overnight at a dog-trot.

You will remember that Mowgli had left the village with the heavy weight of Shere Khan's raw hide on his shoulders, while Akela and Gray Brother trotted behind, so that the triple trail was very clearly marked. Presently Buldeo came to where Akela, as you know, had gone back and mixed it all up. Then he sat down, and coughed and grunted, and made little casts round and about into the Jungle to pick it up again, and, all the time he could have thrown a stone over those who were watching him. No one can be so silent as a wolf when he does not care to be heard; and Mowgli, though the wolves thought he moved very clumsily, could come and go like a shadow. They ringed the old man as a school of porpoises ring a steamer at full speed, and as they ringed him they talked unconcernedly, for their speech began below the lowest end of the scale that untrained human beings can hear. [The other end is bounded by the high squeak of Mang, the Bat, which very many people cannot catch at all. From that note all the bird and bat and insect talk takes on.]

"This is better than any kill," said Gray Brother, as Buldeo stooped and peered and puffed. "He looks like a lost pig in the Jungles by the river. What does he say?" Buldeo was muttering savagely.

Mowgli translated. "He says that packs of wolves must have danced round me. He says that he never saw such a trail in his life. He says he is tired."

"He will be rested before he picks it up again," said Bagheera coolly, as he slipped round a tree-trunk, in the game of blindman's-buff that they were playing. *"Now,* what does the lean thing do?"

"Eat or blow smoke out of his mouth. Men always play with their mouths," said Mowgli; and the silent trailers saw the old man fill and light and puff at a water pipe, and they took good note of the smell of the tobacco, so as to be sure of Buldeo in the darkest night, if necessary.

Then a little knot of charcoal-burners came down the path, and naturally halted to speak to Buldeo, whose fame as a hunter reached for at least twenty miles round. They all sat down and smoked, and Bagheera and the others came up and watched while Buldeo began to tell the story of Mowgli, the Devil-child, from one end to another, with additions and inventions. How he himself had really killed Shere Khan; and how Mowgli had turned himself into a wolf, and fought with him all the afternoon, and changed into a boy again and bewitched Buldeo's rifle, so that the bullet turned the corner, when he pointed it at Mowgli, and killed one of Buldeo's own buffaloes; and how the village, knowing him to be the bravest hunter in Seeonee, had sent him out to kill this Devil-child. But meantime the village had got hold of Messua and her husband, who were undoubtedly the father and mother of this Devil-child, and had barricaded them in their own hut, and presently would torture them to make them confess they were witch and wizard, and then they would be burned to death.

"When?" said the charcoal-burners, because they would very much like to be present at the ceremony.

Buldeo said that nothing would be done till he returned, because the village wished him to kill the

Jungle Boy first. After that they would dispose of Messua and her husband, and divide their lands and buffaloes among the village. Messua's husband had some remarkably fine buffaloes, too. It was an excellent thing to destroy wizards, Buldeo thought; and people who entertained Wolf-children out of the Jungle were clearly the worst kind of witches.

But, said the charcoal-burners, what would happen if the English heard of it? The English, they had heard, were a perfectly mad people, who would not let honest farmers kill witches in peace.

Why, said Buldeo, the head-man of the village would report that Messua and her husband had died of snake-bite. *That* was all arranged, and the only thing now was to kill the Wolf-child. They did not happen to have seen anything of such a creature?

The charcoal-burners looked round cautiously, and thanked their stars they had not; but they had no doubt that so brave a man as Buldeo would find him if anyone could. The sun was getting rather low, and they had an idea that they would push on to Buldeo's village and see that wicked witch. Buldeo said that, though it was his duty to kill the Devil-child, he could not think of letting a party of unarmed men go through the Jungle, which might produce the Wolf-demon at any minute, without his escort. He, therefore, would accompany them, and if the sorcerer's child appeared — well, he would show them how the best hunter in Seeonee dealt with such things. The Brahmin, he said, had given him a charm against the creature that made everything perfectly safe.

"What says he? What says he? What says he?" the wolves repeated every few minutes; and Mowgli translated until he came to the witch part of the story, which was a little beyond him, and then he said that the man and woman who had been so kind to him were trapped.

"Does Man trap Man?" said Bagheera.

"So he says. I cannot understand the talk. They are all mad together. What have Messua and her man to do with me that they should be put in a trap; and what is all this talk about the Red Flower? I must look to this. Whatever they would do to Messua they will not do till Buldeo returns. And so —" Mowgli thought hard, with his fingers playing round the haft of the skinning-knife, while Buldeo and the charcoal-burners went off very valiantly in single file.

"I go hot-foot back to the Man-Pack," Mowgli said at last.

"And those?" said Gray Brother, looking hungrily after the brown backs of the charcoal-burners.

"Sing them home," said Mowgli, with a grin; "I do not wish them to be at the village gates till it is dark. Can ye hold them?"

Gray Brother bared his white teeth in contempt. "We can head them round and round in circles like tethered goats — if I know Man."

"That I do not need. Sing to them a little, lest they be lonely on the road, and, Gray Brother, the song need not be of the sweetest. Go with them, Bagheera, and help make that song. When night is shut down, meet me by the village — Gray Brother knows the place."

"It is no light hunting to work for a Man-cub. When shall I sleep?" said Bagheera, yawning, though his eyes showed that he was delighted with the amusement. "Me to sing to naked men! But let us try."

He lowered his head so that the sound would travel, and cried a long, long, "Good hunting" — a midnight call in the afternoon, which was quite awful enough to begin with. Mowgli heard it rumble, and rise, and fall, and die off in a creepy sort of whine behind him, and laughed to himself as he ran through the Jungle. He could see the charcoal-burners huddled in a knot; old

Buldeo's gun-barrel waving, like a banana-leaf, to every point of the compass at once. Then Gray Brother gave the Ya-la-hi! Yalaha! call for the buck-driving, when the Pack drives the nilghai, the big blue cow, before them, and it seemed to come from the very ends of the earth, nearer, and nearer, and nearer, till it ended in a shriek snapped off short. The other three answered, till even Mowgli could have vowed that the full Pack was in full cry, and then they all broke into the magnificent Morning-song in the Jungle, with every turn, and flourish, and grace-note that a deep-mouthed wolf of the Pack knows. This is a rough rendering of the song, but you must imagine what it sounds like when it breaks the afternoon hush of the Jungle: —

One moment past our bodies cast
    No shadow on the plain;
Now clear and black they stride our track,
    And we run home again.
In morning hush, each rock and bush
    Stands hard, and high, and raw:
Then give the Call: "Good rest to all
    That keep The Jungle Law!"

Now horn and pelt our peoples melt
    In covert to abide;
Now, crouched and still, to cave and hill
    Our Jungle Barons glide.
Now, stark and plain, Man's oxen strain,
    That draw the new-yoked plough;
Now, stripped and dread, the dawn is red
    Above the lit talao.

Ho! Get to lair! The sun's aflare
    Behind the breathing grass:
And cracking through the young bamboo

The warning whispers pass.
By day made strange, the woods we range
  With blinking eyes we scan;
While down the skies the wild duck cries
  "The Day — the Day to Man!"

The dew is dried that drenched our hide
  Or washed about our way;
And where we drank, the puddled bank
  Is crisping into clay.
The traitor Dark gives up each mark
  Of stretched or hooded claw;
Then hear the Call: "Good rest to all
  That keep the Jungle Law!"

But no translation can give the effect of it, or the yelping scorn the Four threw into every word of it, as they heard the trees crash when the men hastily climbed up into the branches, and Buldeo began repeating incantations and charms. Then they lay down and slept, for, like all who live by their own exertions, they were of a methodical cast of mind; and no one can work well without sleep.

Meantime, Mowgli was putting the miles behind him, nine to the hour, swinging on, delighted to find himself so fit after all his cramped months among men. The one idea in his head was to get Messua and her husband out of the trap, whatever it was; for he had a natural mistrust of traps. Later on, he promised himself, he would pay his debts to the village at large.

It was at twilight when he saw the well-remembered grazing-grounds, and the dhak tree where Gray Brother had waited for him on the morning that he killed Shere Khan. Angry as he was at the whole breed and community of Man, something jumped up in his throat and made him catch his breath when he looked at the village roofs. He noticed that everyone had come in from the fields unusually early, and that, instead of getting to their evening cooking, they gathered in a crowd under the village tree, and chattered, and shouted.

"Men must always he making traps for men, or they are not content," said Mowgli. "Last night it was Mowgli — but that night seems many Rains ago. Tonight it is Messua and her man. Tomorrow, and for very many nights after, it will be Mowgli's turn again."

He crept along outside the wall till he came to Messua's hut, and looked through the window into the room. There lay Messua, gagged, and bound hand and foot, breathing hard, and groaning: her husband was tied to the gaily-painted bedstead. The door of the hut that opened into the street was shut fast, and three or four people were sitting with their backs to it.

Mowgli knew the manners and customs of the villagers very fairly. He argued that so long as they could eat, and talk, and smoke, they would not do anything else; but as soon as they had fed they would begin to be dangerous. Buldeo would be coming in before long, and if his escort had done its duty, Buldeo would have a very interesting tale to tell. So he went in through the window, and, stooping over the man and the woman, cut their thongs, pulling out the gags, and looked round the hut for some milk.

Messua was half wild with pain and fear (she had been beaten and stoned all the morning), and Mowgli put his hand over her mouth just in time to stop a scream. Her husband was only bewildered and angry, and sat picking dust and things out of his torn beard.

"I knew — I knew he would come," Messua sobbed at last. "Now do I *know* that he is my son!" and she hugged Mowgli to her heart. Up to that time Mowgli had been perfectly steady, but now he began to tremble all over, and that surprised him immensely.

"Why are these thongs? Why have they tied thee?" he asked, after a pause.

"To be put to the death for making a son of thee — what else?" said the man sullenly. "Look! I bleed."

Messua said nothing, but it was at her wounds that Mowgli looked, and they heard him grit his teeth when he saw the blood.

"Whose work is this?" said he. "There is a price to pay."

"The work of all the village. I was too rich. I had too many cattle. *Therefore* she and I are witches, because we gave thee shelter."

"I do not understand. Let Messua tell the tale."

"I gave thee milk, Nathoo; dost thou remember?" Messua said timidly. "Because thou wast my son, whom the tiger took, and because I loved thee very dearly. They said that I was thy mother, the mother of a devil, and therefore worthy of death."

"And what is a devil?" said Mowgli. "Death I have seen."

The man looked up gloomily, but Messua laughed. "See!" she said to her husband, "I knew — I said that he was no sorcerer. He is my son — my son!"

"Son or sorcerer, what good will that do us?" the man answered. "We be as dead already."

"Yonder is the road to the Jungle" — Mowgli pointed through the window. "Your hands and feet are free. Go now."

"We do not know the Jungle, my son, as — as thou knowest," Messua began. "I do not think that I could walk far."

"And the men and women would be upon our backs and drag us here again," said the husband.

"H'm!" said Mowgli, and he tickled the palm of his hand with the tip of his skinning-knife; "I have no wish to do harm to any one of this village — *yet.* But I do not think they will stay thee. In a little while they will have much else to think upon. Ah!" he lifted his head and listened to shouting and trampling outside. "So they have let Buldeo come home at last?"

"He was sent out this morning to kill thee," Messua cried. "Didst thou meet him?"

"Yes — we — I met him. He has a tale to tell and while he is telling it there is time to do much. But first I will learn what they mean. Think where ye would go, and tell me when I come back."

He bounded through the window and ran along again outside the wall of the village till he came within ear-shot of the crowd round the peepul tree. Buldeo was lying on the ground, coughing and groaning, and everyone was asking him questions. His hair had fallen about his shoulders; his hands and legs were skinned from climbing up trees, and he could hardly speak, but he felt the importance of his position keenly. From time to time he said something about devils and singing devils, and magic enchantment, just to give the crowd a taste of what was coming. Then he called for water.

"Bah!" said Mowgli. "Chatter — chatter! Talk, talk! Men are blood-brothers of the Bandar-log. Now he must wash his mouth with water; now he must blow smoke; and when all that is done he has still his story to tell. They are very wise people — men. They will leave no one to guard Messua till their ears are stuffed with Buldeo's tales. And — I grow as lazy as they!"

He shook himself and glided back to the hut. Just as he was at the window he felt a touch on his foot.

"Mother," said he, for he knew that tongue well, "what dost *thou* here?"

"I heard my children singing through the woods, and I followed the one I loved best. Little Frog, I have a desire to see that woman who gave thee milk," said Mother Wolf, all wet with the dew.

"They have bound and mean to kill her. I have cut those ties, and she goes with her man through the Jungle."

"I also will follow. I am old, but not yet toothless." Mother Wolf reared herself up on end, and looked through the window into the dark of the hut.

In a minute she dropped noiselessly, and all she said was: "I gave thee thy first milk; but Bagheera speaks truth: Man goes to Man at the last."

"Maybe," said Mowgli, with a very unpleasant look on his face; "but tonight I am very far from that trail. Wait here, but do not let her see."

"*Thou* wast never afraid of *me*, Little Frog," said Mother Wolf, backing into the high grass, and blotting herself out, as she knew how.

"And now," said Mowgli cheerfully, as he swung into the hut again, "they are all sitting round Buldeo, who is saying that which did not happen. When his talk is finished, they say they will assuredly come here with the Red — with fire and burn you both. And then?"

"I have spoken to my man," said Messua. Khanhiwara is thirty miles from here, but at Khanhiwara we may find the English — "

"And what Pack are they?" said Mowgli.

"I do not know. They be white, and it is said that they govern all the land, and do not suffer people to burn or beat each other without witnesses. If we can get thither tonight, we live. Otherwise we die."

"Live, then. No man passes the gates tonight. But what does *he* do?" Messua's husband was on his hands and knees digging up the earth in one corner of the hut.

"It is his little money," said Messua. "We can take nothing else."

"Ah, yes. The stuff that passes from hand to hand and never grows warmer. Do they need it outside this place also?" said Mowgli.

The man stared angrily. "He is a fool, and no devil," he muttered. "With the money I can buy a horse. We are too bruised to walk far, and the village will follow us in an hour."

"I say they will *not* follow till I choose; but a horse is well thought of, for Messua is tired." Her husband stood up and knotted the last of the rupees into his waist-cloth. Mowgli helped Messua through the window, and the cool night air revived her, but the Jungle in the starlight looked very dark and terrible.

"Ye know the trail to Khanhiwara?" Mowgli whispered.

They nodded.

"Good. Remember, now, not to be afraid. And there is no need to go quickly. Only — only there may be some small singing in the Jungle behind you and before."

"Think you we would have risked a night in the Jungle through anything less than the fear of burning? It is better to be killed by beasts than by men," said Messua's husband; but Messua looked at Mowgli and smiled.

"I say," Mowgli went on, just as though he were Baloo repeating an old Jungle Law for the hundredth time to a foolish cub — "I say that not a tooth in the Jungle is bared against you; not a foot in the Jungle is lifted against you. Neither man nor beast shall stay you till you come within eye-shot of Khanhiwara. There will be a watch about you." He turned quickly to Messua, saying, "*He* does not believe, but thou wilt believe?"

"Aye, surely, my son. Man, ghost, or wolf of the Jungle, I believe."

"He will be afraid when he hears my people singing. Thou wilt know and understand. Go now, and slowly, for there is no need of any haste. The gates are shut."

Messua flung herself sobbing at Mowgli's feet, but he lifted her very quickly with a shiver. Then she hung about his neck and called him every name of blessing she could think of, but her husband looked enviously across his fields, and said: *"If* we reach Khanhiwara, and I get the ear of the English, I will bring such a lawsuit against the Brahmin and old Buldeo and the others as shall eat the village to the bone. They shall pay me twice over for my crops untilled and my buffaloes unfed. I will have a great justice."

Mowgli laughed. "I do not know what justice is, but — come next Rains. and see what is left."

They went off toward the Jungle, and Mother Wolf leaped from her place of hiding.

"Follow!" said Mowgli; "and look to it that all the Jungle knows these two are safe. Give tongue a little. I would call Bagheera."

The long, low howl rose and fell, and Mowgli saw Messua's husband flinch and turn, half minded to run back to the hut.

"Go on," Mowgli called cheerfully. "I said there might be singing. That call will follow up to Khanhiwara. It is Favor of the Jungle."

Messua urged her husband forward, and the darkness shut down on them and Mother Wolf as Bagheera rose up almost under Mowgli's feet, trembling with delight of the night that drives the Jungle People wild.

"I am ashamed of thy brethren," he said, purring.

"What? Did they not sing sweetly to Buldeo?" said Mowgli.

"Too well! Too well! They made even *me* forget my pride, and, by the Broken Lock that freed me, I went singing through the Jungle as though I were out wooing in the spring! Didst thou not hear us?"

"I had other game afoot. Ask Buldeo if he liked the
song. But where are the Four? I do not wish one of the
Man-Pack to leave the gates tonight."

"What need of the Four, then?" said Bagheera, shifting from foot to foot, his eyes ablaze, and purring
louder than ever. "I can hold them, Little Brother. Is
it killing at last? The singing and the sight of the men
climbing up the trees have made me very ready. Who
is Man that we should care for him — the naked brown
digger, the hairless and toothless, the eater of earth? I
have followed him all day — at noon — in the white
sunlight. I herded him as the wolves herd buck. I am
Bagheera! Bagheera! Bagheera! As I dance with my
shadow, so danced I with those men. Look!" The great
panther leaped as a kitten leaps at a dead leaf whirling
overhead, struck left and right into the empty air, that
sang under the strokes, landed noiselessly, and leaped
again and again, while the half purr, half growl gathered head as steam rumbles in a boiler. "I am Bagheera
— in the jungle — in the night, and my strength is in
me. Who shall stay my stroke? Man-cub, with one blow
of my paw I could beat thy head flat as a dead frog in
the summer!"

"Strike, then!" said Mowgli, in the dialect of the
village, *not* the talk of the Jungle, and the human words
brought Bagheera to a full stop, flung back on
haunches that quivered under him, his head just at the
level of Mowgli's. Once more Mowgli stared, as he had
stared at the rebellious cubs, full into the beryl-green
eyes till the red glare behind their green went out like
the light of a lighthouse shut off twenty miles across
the sea; till the eyes dropped, and the big head with
them — dropped lower and lower, and the red rasp of
a tongue grated on Mowgli's instep.

"Brother — Brother — Brother!" the boy whispered,

stroking steadily and lightly from the neck along the heaving back. "Be still, be still! It is the fault of the night, and no fault of thine."

"It was the smells of the night," said Bagheera penitently. "This air cries aloud to me. But how dost *thou* know?"

Of course the air round an Indian village is full of all kinds of smells, and to any creature who does nearly all his thinking through his nose, smells are as maddening as music and drugs are to human beings. Mowgli gentled the panther for a few minutes longer, and he lay down like a cat before a fire, his paws tucked under his breast, and his eyes half shut.

"Thou art of the Jungle and *not* of the Jungle," he said at last. "And I am only a black panther. But I love thee, Little Brother."

"They are very long at their talk under the tree," Mowgli said, without noticing the last sentence. "Buldeo must have told many tales. They should come soon to drag the woman and her man out of the trap and put them into the Red Flower. They will find that trap sprung. Ho! ho!"

"Nay, listen," said Bagheera. "The fever is out of my blood now. Let them find *me* there! Few would leave their houses after meeting me. It is not the first time I have been in a cage; and I do not think they will tie *me* with cords."

"Be wise, then," said Mowgli, laughing; for he was beginning to feel as reckless as the panther, who had glided into the hut.

"Pah!" Bagheera grunted. "This place is rank with Man, but here is just such a bed as they gave me to lie upon in the King's cages at Oodeypore. Now I lie down." Mowgli heard the strings of the cot crack under the great brute's weight. "By the Broken Lock that freed me, they will think they have caught big game! Come and sit beside me, Little Brother; we will give them 'good hunting' together!"

"No; I have another thought in my stomach. The Man-Pack shall not know what share I have in the sport. Make thine own hunt. I do not wish to see them."

"Be it so," said Bagheera. "Ah, now they come!"

The conference under the peepul tree had been growing noisier and noisier, at the far end of the village. It broke in wild yells, and a rush up the street of men and women, waving clubs and bamboos and sickles and knives. Buldeo and the Brahmin were at the head of it, but the mob was close at their heels, and they cried, "The witch and the wizard! Let us see if hot coins will make them confess! Burn the hut over their heads! We will teach them to shelter wolf-devils! Nay, beat them first! Torches! More torches! Buldeo, heat the gun-barrels!"

Here was some little difficulty with the catch of the door. It had been very firmly fastened, but the crowd tore it away bodily, and the light of the torches streamed into the room where, stretched at full length on the bed, his paws crossed and lightly hung down over one end, black as the Pit, and terrible as a demon, was Bagheera. There was one half-minute of desperate silence, as the front ranks of the crowd clawed and tore their way back from the threshold, and in that minute Bagheera raised his head and yawned — elaborately, carefully, and ostentatiously — as he would yawn when he wished to insult an equal. The fringed lips drew back and up; the red tongue curled; the lower jaw dropped and dropped till you could see half-way down the hot gullet; and the gigantic dog-teeth stood clear to the pit of the gums till they rang together, upper and under, with the snick of steel-faced wards shooting home round the edges of a safe. Next instant the street was empty; Bagheera had leaped back through the window, and stood at Mowgli's side, while a yelling, screaming torrent scrambled and tumbled one over another in their panic haste to get to their own huts.

"They will not stir till day comes," said Bagheera quietly. "And now?"

The silence of the afternoon sleep seemed to have overtaken the village; but, as they listened, they could hear the sound of heavy grain-boxes being dragged over earthen floors and set down against doors. Bagheera was quite right; the village would not stir till daylight. Mowgli sat still, and thought, and his face grew darker and darker.

"What have I done?" said Bagheera, at last coming to his feet, fawning.

"Nothing but great good. Watch them now till the day. I sleep." Mowgli ran off into the Jungle, and dropped like a dead man across a rock, and slept and slept the day round, and the night back again.

When he waked, Bagheera was at his side, and there was a newly-killed buck at his feet. Bagheera watched curiously while Mowgli went to work with his skinning-knife, ate and drank, and turned over with his chin in his hands.

"The man and the woman are come safe within eye-shot of Khanhiwara," Bagheera said. "Thy lair mother sent the word back by Chil, the Kite. They found a horse before midnight of the night they were freed, and went very quickly. Is not that well?"

"That is well," said Mowgli.

"And thy Man-Pack in the village did not stir till the sun was high this morning. Then they ate their food and ran back quickly to their houses."

"Did they, by chance, see thee?"

"It may have been. I was rolling in the dust before the gate at dawn, and I may have made also some small song to myself. Now, Little Brother, there is nothing more to do. Come hunting with me and Baloo. He has new hives that he wishes to show, and we all desire thee back again as of old. Take off that look which makes even me afraid! The man and woman will not be put into the Red Flower, and all goes well in the Jungle. Is it not true? Let us forget the Man-Pack."

"They shall he forgotten in a little while. Where does Hathi feed tonight?"

"Where he chooses. Who can answer for the Silent One? But why? What is there Hathi can do which we cannot?"

"Bid him and his three sons come here to me."

"But, indeed, and truly, Little Brother, it is not — it is not seemly to say 'Come,' and 'Go,' to Hathi. Remember, he is the Master of the Jungle, and before the Man-Pack changed the look on thy face, he taught thee the Master-words of the Jungle."

"That is all one. I have a Master-word for him now. Bid him come to Mowgli, the Frog: and if he does not hear at first, bid him come because of the Sack of the Fields of Bhurtpore."

"The Sack of the Fields of Bhurtpore," Bagheera repeated two or three times to make sure. "I go. Hathi can but be angry at the worst, and I would give a moon's hunting to hear a Master-word that compels the Silent One."

He went away, leaving Mowgli stabbing furiously with his skinning-knife into the earth. Mowgli had never seen human blood in his life before till he had seen, and — what meant much more to him — smelled Messua's blood on the thongs that bound her. And Messua had been kind to him, and, so far as he knew anything about love, he loved Messua as completely as he hated the rest of mankind. But deeply as he loathed them, their talk, their cruelty, and their cowardice, not for anything the Jungle had to offer could he bring himself to take a human life, and have that terrible scent of blood back again in his nostrils. His plan was simpler, but much more thorough; and he laughed to himself when he thought that it was one of old Buldeo's tales told under the peepul tree in the evening that had put the idea into his head.

"It *was* a Master-word," Bagheera whispered in his ear. "They were feeding by the river, and they obeyed as though they were bullocks. Look where they come now!"

Hathi and his three sons had arrived, in their usual way, without a sound. The mud of the river was still fresh on their flanks, and Hathi was thoughtfully chewing the green stem of a young plantain tree that he had gouged up with his tusks. But every line in his vast body showed to Bagheera, who could see things when he came across them, that it was not the Master of the Jungle speaking to a Man-cub, but one who was afraid coming before one who was not. His three sons rolled side by side, behind their father.

Mowgli hardly lifted his head as Hathi gave him "Good hunting." He kept him swinging and rocking, and shifting from one foot to another, for a long time before he spoke; and when he opened his mouth it was to Bagheera, not to the elephants.

"I will tell a tale that was told to me by the hunter ye hunted today," said Mowgli. "It concerns an elephant, old and wise, who fell into a trap, and the sharpened stake in the pit scarred him from a little above his heel to the crest of his shoulder, leaving a white mark." Mowgli threw out his hand, and as Hathi wheeled the moonlight showed a long white scar on his slaty side, as though he had been struck with a red-hot whip. "Men came to take him from the trap," Mowgli continued, "but he broke his ropes, for he was strong, and went away till his wound was healed. Then came he, angry, by night to the fields of those hunters. And I remember now that he had three sons. These things happened many, many Rains ago, and very far away — among the fields of Bhurtpore. What came to those fields at the next reaping, Hathi?"

"They were reaped by me and by my three sons," said Hathi.

"And to the ploughing that follows the reaping?" said Mowgli.

"There was no ploughing," said Hathi.

"And to the men that live by the green crops on the ground?" said Mowgli.

"They went away."

"And to the huts in which the men slept?" said Mowgli.

"We tore the roofs to pieces, and the Jungle swallowed up the walls," said Hathi.

"And what more?" said Mowgli.

"As much good ground as I can walk over in two nights from the east to the west, and from the north to the south as much as I can walk over in three nights, the Jungle took. We let in the Jungle upon five villages; and in those villages, and in their lands, the grazing-ground and the soft crop-grounds, there is not one man today who takes his food from the ground. That was the Sack of the Fields of Bhurtpore, which I and my three sons did; and now I ask, Man-cub, how the news of it came to thee?" said Hathi.

"A man told me, and now I see even Buldeo can speak truth. It was well done, Hathi with the white mark; but the second time it shall be done better, for the reason that there is a man to direct. Thou knowest the village of the Man-Pack that cast me out? They are idle, senseless, and cruel; they play with their mouths, and they do not kill the weaker for food, but for sport.

When they are full-fed they would throw their own breed into the Red Flower. This I have seen. It is not well that they should live here anymore. I hate them!"

"Kill, then," said the youngest of Hathi's three sons, picking up a tuft of grass, dusting it against his forelegs, and throwing it away, while his little red eyes glanced furtively from side to side.

"What good are white bones to me?" Mowgli answered angrily. "Am I the cub of a wolf to play in the sun with a raw head? I have killed Shere Khan, and his hide rots on the Council Rock; but — but I do not know whither Shere Khan is gone, and my stomach is still empty. Now I will take that which I can see and touch. Let in the Jungle upon that village, Hathi!"

Bagheera shivered, and cowered down. He could understand, if the worst came to the worst, a quick rush down the village street, and a right and left blow into a crowd, or a crafty killing of men as they ploughed in the twilight; but this scheme for deliberately blotting out an entire village from the eyes of man and beast frightened him. Now he saw why Mowgli had sent for Hathi. No one but the long-lived elephant could plan and carry through such a war.

"Let them run as the men ran from the fields of Bhurtpore, till we have the rain-water for the only plough, and the noise of the rain on the thick leaves for the pattering of their spindles — till Bagheera and I lair in the house of the Brahmin, and the buck drink at the tank behind the temple! Let in the Jungle, Hathi!"

"But I — but we have no quarrel with them, and it needs the red rage of great pain ere we tear down the places where men sleep," said Hathi doubtfully.

"Are ye the only eaters of grass in the Jungle? Drive in your peoples. Let the deer and the pig and the nilghai look to it. Ye need never show a hand's-breadth of hide till the fields are naked. Let in the Jungle, Hathi!"

"There will be no killing? My tusks were red at the Sack of the Fields of Bhurtpore, and I would not wake that smell again."

"Nor I. I do not wish even their bones to lie on the clean earth. Let them go and find a fresh lair. They cannot stay here. I have seen and smelled the blood of the woman that gave me food – the woman whom they would have killed but for me. Only the smell of the new grass on their doorsteps can take away that smell. It burns in my mouth. Let in the Jungle, Hathi!"

"Ah!" said Hathi. "So did the scar of the stake burn on my hide till we watched the villages die under in the spring growth. Now I see. Thy war shall he our war. We will let in the jungle!"

Mowgli had hardly time to catch his breath – he was shaking all over with rage and hate before the place where the elephants had stood was empty, and Bagheera was looking at him with terror.

"By the Broken Lock that freed me!" said the Black Panther at last. "Art *thou* the naked thing I spoke for in the Pack when all was young? Master of the Jungle, when my strength goes, speak for me – speak for Baloo – speak for us all! We are cubs before thee! Snapped twigs under foot! Fawns that have lost their doe!"

The idea of Bagheera being a stray fawn upset Mowgli altogether, and he laughed and caught his breath, and sobbed and laughed again, till he had to jump into a pool to make himself stop. Then he swam round and round, ducking in and out of the bars of the moonlight like the frog, his namesake.

By this time Hathi and his three sons had turned, each to one point of the compass, and were striding silently down the valleys a mile away. They went on and on for two days' march – that is to say, a long sixty miles – through the Jungle; and every step they took, and every wave of their trunks, was known and noted and talked over by Mang and Chil and the Monkey People and all the birds. Then they began to feed, and fed quietly for a week or so. Hathi and his sons are like Kaa, the Rock Python. They never hurry till they have to.

At the end of that time – and none knew who had started it – a rumor went through the Jungle that there was better food and water to be found in such and such a valley. The pig – who, of course, will go to the ends of the earth for a full meal – moved first by companies, scuffling over the rocks, and the deer followed, with the small wild foxes that live on the dead and dying of the herds; and the heavy-shouldered nilghai moved parallel with the deer, and the wild buffaloes of the swamps came after the nilghai. The least little thing would have turned the scattered, straggling droves that grazed and sauntered and drank and grazed again; but whenever there was an alarm some one would rise up and soothe them. At one time it would be Ikki the Porcupine, full of news of good feed just a little farther on; at another Mang would cry cheerily and flap down a glade to show it was all empty; or Baloo, his mouth full of roots, would shamble alongside a wavering line and half frighten, half romp it clumsily back to the proper road. Very many creatures broke back or ran away or lost interest, but very many were left to go forward. At the end of another ten days or so the situation was this. The deer and the pig and the nilghai were milling round and round in a circle of eight or ten miles radius, while the Eaters of Flesh skirmished round its edge. And the center of that circle was the village, and round the village the crops were ripening, and in the crops sat men on what they call machans – platforms like pigeon-perches, made of sticks at the top of four poles — to scare away birds and other stealers. Then the deer were coaxed no more. The Eaters of Flesh were close behind them, and forced them forward and inward.

It was a dark night when Hathi and his three sons slipped down from the Jungle, and broke off the poles of the machans with their trunks; they fell as a snapped stalk of hemlock in bloom falls, and the men that tumbled from them heard the deep gurgling of the elephants in their ears. Then the vanguard of the be-wildered armies of the deer broke down and flooded into the village grazing-grounds and the ploughed fields; and the sharp-hoofed, rooting wild pig came with them, and what the deer left the pig spoiled, and from time to time an alarm of wolves would shake the herds, and they would rush to and fro desperately, treading down the young barley, and cutting flat the banks of the irrigating channels. Before the dawn broke the pressure on the outside of the circle gave way at one point. The Eaters of Flesh had fallen back and left an open path to the south, and drove upon drove of buck fled along it. Others, who were bolder, lay up in the thickets to finish their meal next night.

But the work was practically done. When the villag-ers looked in the morning they saw their crops were lost. And that meant death if they did not get away, for they lived year in and year out as near to starvation as the Jungle was near to them. When the buffaloes were sent to graze the hungry brutes found that the deer had cleared the grazing-grounds, and so wandered into the Jungle and drifted off with their wild mates; and when twilight fell the three or four ponies that belonged to the village lay in their stables with their heads beaten in. Only Bagheera could have given those strokes, and only Bagheera would have thought of insolently dragging the last carcass to the open street.

The villagers had no heart to make fires in the fields
that night, so Hathi and his three sons went gleaning
among what was left; and where Hathi gleans there is
no need to follow. The men decided to live on their
stored seed-corn until the rains had fallen, and then to
take work as servants till they could catch up with the
lost year; but as the grain-dealer was thinking of his
well-filled crates of corn, and the prices he would levy
at the sale of it, Hathi's sharp tusks were picking out
the corner of his mud-house, and smashing open the
big wicker chest, leeped with cow-dung, where the
precious stuff lay.

When that last loss was discovered, it was the Brahmin's turn to speak. He had prayed to his own Gods
without answer. It might be, he said, that, unconsciously, the village had offended some one of the
Gods of the Jungle, for, beyond doubt, the Jungle was
against them. So they sent for the head-man of the
nearest tribe of wandering Gonds — little, wise, and
very black hunters, living in the deep Jungle, whose
fathers came of the oldest race in India — the aboriginal
owners of the land. They made the Gond welcome with
what they had, and he stood on one leg, his bow in his
hand, and two or three poisoned arrows stuck through
his top-knot, looking half afraid and half contemptuously at the anxious villagers and their ruined fields.
They wished to know whether his Gods — the Old Gods
— were angry with them and what sacrifices should be
offered. The Gond said nothing, but picked up a trail
of the Karela, the vine that bears the bitter wild gourd,
and laced it to and fro across the temple door in the
face of the staring red Hindu image. Then he pushed
with his hand in the open air along the road to Khanhiwara, and went back to his Jungle, and watched the
Jungle People drifting through it. He knew that when
the Jungle moves only white men can hope to turn it

aside.

There was no need to ask his meaning. The wild gourd would grow where they had worshipped their God, and the sooner they saved themselves the better.

But it is hard to tear a village from its moorings. They stayed on as long as any summer food was left to them, and they tried to gather nuts in the Jungle, but shadows with glaring eyes watched them, and rolled before them even at mid-day; and when they ran back afraid to their walls, on the tree-trunks they had passed not five minutes before the bark would be stripped and chiselled with the stroke of some great taloned paw. The more they kept to their village, the bolder grew the wild things that gambolled and bellowed on the grazing-grounds by the Waingunga. They had no time to patch and plaster the rear walls of the empty byres that backed on to the Jungle; the wild pig trampled them down, and the knotty-rooted vines hurried after and threw their elbows over the new-won ground, and the coarse grass bristled behind the vines like the lances of a goblin army following a retreat. The unmarried men ran away first, and carried the news far and near that the village was doomed. Who could fight, they said, against the Jungle, or the Gods of the Jungle, when the very village cobra had left his hole in the platform under the peepul tree? So their little commerce with the outside world shrunk as the trodden paths across the open grew fewer and fainter. At last the nightly trumpetings of Hathi and his three sons ceased to trouble them; for they had no more to be robbed of. The crop on the ground and the seed in the ground had been taken. The outlying fields were already losing their shape, and it was time to throw themselves on the charity of the English at Khanhiwara.

Native fashion, they delayed their departure from one day to another till the first Rains caught them and the unmended roofs let in a flood, and the grazing-ground stood ankle deep, and all life came on with a rush after the heat of the summer. Then they waded out — men, women, and children — through the blinding hot rain of the morning, but turned naturally for one farewell look at their homes.

They heard, as the last burdened family filed through the gate, a crash of falling beams and thatch behind the walls. They saw a shiny, snaky black trunk lifted for an instant, scattering sodden thatch. It disappeared, and there was another crash, followed by a squeal. Hathi had been plucking off the roofs of the huts as you pluck water-lilies, and a rebounding beam had pricked him. He needed only this to unchain his full strength, for of all things in the Jungle the wild elephant enraged is the most wantonly destructive. He kicked backward at a mud wall that crumbled at the stroke, and, crumbling, melted to yellow mud under the torrent of rain. Then he wheeled and squealed, and tore through the narrow streets, leaning against the huts right and left, shivering the crazy doors, and crumpling up the caves; while his three sons raged behind as they had raged at the Sack of the Fields of Bhurtpore.

"The Jungle will swallow these shells," said a quiet voice in the wreckage. "It is the outer wall that must lie down," and Mowgli, with the rain sluicing over his bare shoulders and arms, leaped back from a wall that was settling like a tired buffalo.

"All in good time," panted Hathi. "Oh, but my tusks were red at Bhurtpore; To the outer wall, children! With the head! Together! Now!"

The four pushed side by side; the outer wall bulged, split, and fell, and the villagers, dumb with horror, saw the savage, clay-streaked heads of the wreckers in the ragged gap. Then they fled, houseless and foodless, down the valley, as their village, shredded and tossed and trampled, melted behind them.

A month later the place was a dimpled mound, covered with soft, green young stuff; and by the end of the Rains there was the roaring jungle in full blast on the spot that had been under plough not six months before.

Mowgli's Song against People

I will let loose against you the fleet-footed vines —
I will call in the Jungle to stamp out your lines!
    The roofs shall fade before it,
    The house-beams shall fall,
    And the Karela, the bitter Karela,
    Shall cover it all!

In the gates of these your councils my people shall
    sing,
In the doors of these your garners the Bat-folk shall
    cling;
    And the snake shall be your watchman,
    By a hearthstone unswept;
    For the Karela, the bitter Karela,
    Shall fruit where ye slept!

Ye shall not see my strikers; ye shall hear them and
    guess;
By night, before the moon-rise, I will send for my

cess,
And the wolf shall he your herdsman
   By a landmark removed,
For the Karela, the bitter Karela,
   Shall seed where ye loved!

I will reap your fields before you at the hands of a
      host;
Ye shall glean behind my reapers, for the bread that
      is lost,
   And the deer shall be your oxen
      By a headland untilled,
For the Karela, the bitter Karela,
   Shall leaf where ye build!

I have untied against you the club-footed vines,
I have sent in the Jungle to swamp out your lines.
   The trees — the trees are on you!
   The house-beams shall fall,
   And the Karela, the bitter Karela,
      Shall cover you all!

The Undertakers

When ye say to Tabaqui, "My Brother!" when ye call
    the Hyena to meat,
Ye may cry the Full Truce with Jacala — the Belly
    that runs on four feet.
                           Jungle Law

"*R*espect the aged!"

"It was a thick voice — a muddy voice that would
have made you shudder — a voice like something soft
breaking in two. There was a quaver in it, a croak and
a whine.

"Respect the aged! O Companions of the River —
respect the aged!"

Nothing could be seen on the broad reach of the
river except a little fleet of square-sailed, wooden-
pinned barges, loaded with building-stone, that had
just come under the railway bridge, and were driving
down-stream. They put their clumsy helms over to
avoid the sand-bar made by the scour of the bridge-
piers, and as they passed, three abreast, the horrible
voice began again:

"O Brahmins of the River — respect the aged and

infirm!"

A boatman turned where he sat on the gunwale, lifted up his hand, said something that was not a blessing, and the boats creaked on through the twilight. The broad Indian river, that looked more like a chain of little lakes than a stream, was as smooth as glass, reflecting the sandy-red sky in mid-channel, but splashed with patches of yellow and dusky purple near and under the low banks. Little creeks ran into the river in the wet season, but now their dry mouths hung clear above water-line. On the left shore, and almost under the railway bridge, stood a mud-and-brick and thatch-and-stick village, whose main street, full of cattle going back to their byres, ran straight to the river, and ended in a sort of rude brick pier-head, where people who wanted to wash could wade in step by step. That was the Ghaut of the village of Mugger-Ghaut.

Night was falling fast over the fields of lentils and rice and cotton in the low-lying ground yearly flooded by the river; over the reeds that fringed the elbow of the bend, and the tangled jungle of the grazing-grounds behind the still reeds. The parrots and crows, who had been chattering and shouting over their evening drink, had flown inland to roost, crossing the out-going battalions of the flying-foxes; and cloud upon cloud of water-birds came whistling and "honking" to the cover of the reed-beds. There were geese, barrel-headed and black-backed, teal, widgeon, mallard, and sheldrake, with curlews, and here and there a flamingo.

A lumbering Adjutant-crane brought up the rear, flying as though each slow stroke would be his last.

"Respect the aged! Brahmins of the River — respect the aged!"

The Adjutant half turned his head, sheered a little in the direction of the voice, and landed stiffly on the sand-bar below the bridge. Then you saw what a ruffianly brute he really was. His back view was immensely respectable, for he stood nearly six feet high, and looked rather like a very proper bald-headed parson. In front it was different, for his Ally Sloperlike head and neck had not a feather to them, and there was a horrible raw-skin pouch on his neck under his chin — a hold-all for the things his pick-axe beak might steal. His legs were long and thin and skinny, but he moved them delicately, and looked at them with pride as he preened down his ashy-gray tail-feathers, glanced over the smooth of his shoulder, and stiffened into "Stand at attention."

A mangy little Jackal, who had been yapping hungrily on a low bluff, cocked up his ears and tail, and scuttered across the shallows to join the Adjutant.

He was the lowest of his caste — not that the best of jackals are good for much, but this one was peculiarly low, being half a beggar, half a criminal — a cleaner-up of village rubbish-heaps, desperately timid or wildly bold, everlastingly hungry, and full of cunning that never did him any good.

"Ugh!" he said, shaking himself dolefully as he landed. "May the red mange destroy the dogs of this village! I have three bites for each flea upon me, and all because I looked — only looked, mark you — at an old shoe in a cow-byre. Can I eat mud?" He scratched himself under his left ear.

"I heard," said the Adjutant, in a voice like a blunt saw going through a thick board — "I *heard* there was a newborn puppy in that same shoe."

"To hear is one thing; to know is another," said the Jackal, who had a very fair knowledge of proverbs, picked up by listening to men round the village fires of an evening.

"Quite true. So, to make sure, I took care of that puppy while the dogs were busy elsewhere."

"They were *very* busy," said the Jackal. "Well, I must not go to the village hunting for scraps yet awhile. And so there truly was a blind puppy in that shoe?"

"It is here," said the Adjutant, squinting over his beak at his full pouch. "A small thing, but acceptable now that charity is dead in the world."

"Ahai! The world is iron in these days," wailed the Jackal. Then his restless eye caught the least possible ripple on the water, and he went on quickly: "Life is hard for us all, and I doubt not that even our excellent master, the Pride of the Ghaut and the Envy of the River —"

"A liar, a flatterer, and a Jackal were all hatched out of the same egg," said the Adjutant to nobody in particular; for he was rather a fine sort of a liar on his own account when he took the trouble.

"Yes, the Envy of the River," the Jackal repeated, raising his voice. "Even he, I doubt not, finds that since the bridge has been built good food is more scarce. But on the other hand, though I would by no means say this to his noble face, he is so wise and so virtuous — as I, alas I am not —"

"When the Jackal owns he is gray, how black must the Jackal be!" muttered the Adjutant. He could not see what was coming.

"That his food never fails, and in consequence —"

There was a soft grating sound, as though a boat had just touched in shoal water. The Jackal spun round quickly and faced (it is always best to face) the creature he had been talking about. It was a twenty-four-foot crocodile, cased in what looked like treble-riveted boiler-plate, studded and keeled and crested; the yellow points of his upper teeth just overhanging his beautifully fluted lower jaw. It was the blunt-nosed Mugger of Mugger-Ghaut, older than any man in the village, who had given his name to the village; the demon of the ford before the railway bridge, came — murderer, man-eater, and local fetish in one. He lay with his chin in the shallows, keeping his place by an almost invisible rippling of his tail, and well the Jackal knew that one stroke of that same tail in the water would carry the Mugger up the bank with the rush of a steam-engine.

"Auspiciously met, Protector of the Poor!" he fawned, backing at every word. "A delectable voice was heard, and we came in the hopes of sweet conversation. My tailless presumption, while waiting here, led me, indeed, to speak of thee. It is my hope that nothing was overheard."

Now the Jackal had spoken just to be listened to, for he knew flattery was the best way of getting things to eat, and the Mugger knew that the Jackal had spoken for this end, and the Jackal knew that the Mugger knew, and the Mugger knew that the Jackal knew that the Mugger knew, and so they were all very contented together.

The old brute pushed and panted and grunted up the bank, mumbling, "Respect the aged and infirm!" and all the time his little eyes burned like coals under the heavy, horny eyelids on the top of his triangular head, as he shoved his bloated barrel-body along between his crutched legs. Then he settled down, and, accustomed as the Jackal was to his ways, he could not help starting, for the hundredth time, when he saw how exactly the Mugger imitated a log adrift on the bar. He had even taken pains to lie at the exact angle a naturally stranded log would make with the water, having regard to the current of

he season at the time and place. All this was only a matter of habit, of course, because the Mugger had come ashore for pleasure; but a crocodile is never quite full, and if the Jackal had been deceived by the likeness he would not have lived to philosophise over it.

"My child, I heard nothing," said the Mugger, shutting one eye. "The water was in my ears, and also I was faint with hunger. Since the railway bridge was built my people at my village have ceased to love me; and that is breaking my heart."

"Ah, shame!" said the Jackal. "So noble a heart, too! But men are all alike, to my mind."

"Nay, there are very great differences indeed," the Mugger answered gently. "Some are as lean asboat-poles. Others again are fat as young ja — dogs. Never would I causelessly revile men. They are of all fashions, but the long years have shown me that, one with another, they are very good. Men, women, and children — I have no fault to find with them. And remember, child, he who rebukes the World is rebuked by the World."

"Flattery is worse than an empty tin can in the belly. But that which we have just heard is wisdom," said the Adjutant, bringing down one foot.

"Consider, though, their ingratitude to this excellent one," began the Jackal tenderly.

"Nay, nay, not ingratitude!" the Mugger said. "They do not think for others; that is all. But I have noticed, lying at my station below the ford, that the stairs of the new bridge are cruelly hard to climb, both for old people and young children. The old, indeed, are not so worthy of consideration, but I am grieved — I am truly grieved — on account of the fat children. Still, I think, in a little while, when the newness of the bridge has worn away, we shall see my people's bare brown legs bravely splashing through the ford as before. Then the old Mugger will be honored again."

"But surely I saw Marigold wreaths floating off the edge of the Ghaut only this noon," said the Adjutant.

Marigold wreaths are a sign of reverence all India

over.

"An error — an error. It was the wife of the sweet-meat-seller. She loses her eyesight year by year, and cannot tell a log from me — the Mugger of the Ghaut. I saw the mistake when she threw the garland, for I was lying at the very foot of the Ghaut, and had she taken another step I might have shown her some little difference. Yet she meant well, and we must consider the spirit of the offering."

"What good are marigold wreaths when one is on the rubbish-heap?" said the Jackal, hunting for fleas, but keeping one wary eye on his Protector of the Poor.

"True, but they have not yet begun to make the rubbish-heap that shall carry *me*. Five times have I seen the river draw back from the village and make new land at the foot of the street. Five times have I seen the village rebuilt on the banks, and I shall see it built yet five times more. I am no faithless, fish-hunting Gavial, I, at Kasi today and Prayag tomorrow, as the saying is, but the true and constant watcher of the ford. It is not for nothing, child, that the village bears my name, and 'he who watches long,' as the saying is, 'shall at last have his reward.'"

"*I* have watched long — very long — nearly all my life, and my reward has been bites and blows," said the Jackal.

"Ho! ho! ho!" roared the Adjutant.

"In August was the Jackal born;
    The Rains fell in September;
'Now such a fearful flood as this,'
    Says he, 'I can't remember!'"

There is one very unpleasant peculiarity about the Adjutant. At uncertain times he suffers from acute attacks of the fidgets or cramp in his legs, and though he is more virtuous to behold than any of the cranes, who are all immensely respectable, he flies off into wild, cripple-stilt war-dances, half opening his wings and bobbing his bald head up and down; while for reasons best known to himself he is very careful to time his worst attacks with his nastiest remarks. At the last word of his song he came to attention again, ten times adjutaunter than before.

The Jackal winced, though he was full three seasons old, but you cannot resent an insult from a person with a beak a yard long, and the power of driving it like a javelin. The Adjutant was a most notorious coward, but the Jackal was worse.

"We must live before we can learn," said the Mugger, "and there is this to say: Little jackals are very common, child, but such a mugger as I am is not common. For all that, I am not proud, since pride is destruction; but take notice, it is Fate, and against his Fate no one who swims or walks or runs should say anything at all. I am well contented with Fate. With good luck, a keen eye, and the custom of considering whether a creek or a backwater has an outlet to it ere you ascend, much may be done."

"Once I heard that even the Protector of the Poor made a mistake," said the Jackal viciously.

"True; but there my Fate helped me. It was before I had come to my full growth — before the last famine but three (by the Right and Left of Gunga, how full used the streams to be in those days!). Yes, I was young and unthinking, and when the flood came, who so pleased as I? A little made me very happy then. The village was deep in flood, and I swam above the Ghaut and went far inland, up to the rice-fields, and they were deep in good mud. I remember also a pair of bracelets (glass they were, and troubled me not a little) that I found that evening. Yes, glass bracelets; and, if my memory serves me well, a shoe. I should have shaken off both shoes, but I was hungry. I learned better later. Yes. And so I fed and rested me; but when I was ready to go to the river again the flood had fallen, and I walked through the mud of the main street. Who but I? Came out all my people, priests and women and children, and I looked upon them with benevolence. The mud is not a good place to fight in. Said a boatman, 'Get axes and kill him, for he is the Mugger of the ford.' 'Not so,' said the Brahmin. 'Look, he is driving the flood before him! He is the godling of the village.' Then they threw many flowers at me, and by happy thought one led a goat across the road.'

"How good — how very good is goat!" said the Jackal.

"Hairy — too hairy, and when found in the water more than likely to hide a cross-shaped hook. But that goat I accepted, and went down to the Ghaut in great honor. Later, my Fate sent me the boatman who had desired to cut off my tail with an axe. His boat grounded upon an old shoal which you would not remember."

"We are not *all* jackals here," said the Adjutant. "Was it the shoal made where the stone-boats sank in the year of the great drouth — a long shoal that lasted three floods?"

"There were two," said the Mugger; "an upper and a lower shoal."

"Aye, I forgot. A channel divided them, and later dried up again," said the Adjutant, who prided himself on his memory.

"On the lower shoal my well-wisher's craft grounded. He was sleeping in the bows, and, half awake, leaped over to his waist — no, it was no more than to his knees — to push off. His empty boat went on and touched again below the next reach, as the river ran then. I followed, because I knew men would come out to drag it ashore."

"And did they do so?" said the Jackal, a little awe-stricken. This was hunting on a scale that impressed him.

"There and lower down they did. I went no farther, but that gave me three in one day — well-fed manjis (boatmen) all, and, except in the case of the last (then I was careless), never a cry to warn those on the bank."

"Ah, noble sport! But what cleverness and great judgment it requires!" said the Jackal.

"Not cleverness, child, but only thought. A little thought in life is like salt upon rice, as the boatmen say, and I have thought deeply always. The Gavial, my cousin, the fish-eater, has told me how hard it is for him to follow his fish, and how one fish differs from the other, and how he must know them all, both together and apart. I say that is wisdom; but, on the other hand, my cousin, the Gavial, lives among his people. *My* people do not swim in companies, with their mouths out of the water, as Rewa does; nor do they constantly rise to the surface of the water, and turn over on their sides, like Mohoo and little Chapta; nor do they gather in shoals after flood, like Batchua and Chilwa."

"All are very good eating," said the Adjutant, clattering his beak.

"So my cousin says, and makes a great to-do over hunting them, but they do not climb the banks to escape his sharp nose. *My* people are otherwise. Their life is on the land, in the houses, among the cattle. I must know what they do, and what they are about to do; and adding the tail to the trunk, as the saying is, I make up the whole elephant. Is there a green branch and an iron ring hanging over a doorway? The old Mugger knows that a boy has been born in that house, and must some day come down to the Ghaut to play.

Is a maiden to be married? The old Mugger knows, for he sees the men carry gifts back and forth; and she, too, comes down to the Ghaut to bathe before her wedding, and — he is there. Has the river changed its channel, and made new land where there was only sand before? The Mugger knows."

"Now, of what use is that knowledge?" said the Jackal. "The river has shifted even in my little life." Indian rivers are nearly always moving about in their beds, and will shift, sometimes, as much as two or three miles in a season, drowning the fields on one bank, and spreading good silt on the other.

"There is no knowledge so useful," said the Mugger, "for new land means new quarrels. The Mugger knows. Oho! the Mugger knows. As soon as the water has drained off, he creeps up the little creeks that men think would not hide a dog, and there he waits. Presently comes a farmer saying he will plant cucumbers here, and melons there, in the new land that the river has given him. He feels the good mud with his bare toes. Anon comes another, saying he will put onions, and carrots, and sugar-cane in such and such places. They meet as boats adrift meet, and each rolls his eye at the other under the big blue turban. The old Mugger sees and hears. Each calls the other 'Brother,' and they go to mark out the boundaries of the new land. The Mugger hurries with them from point to point, shuffling very low through the mud. Now they begin to quarrel! Now they say hot words! Now they pull turbans! Now they lift up their lathis (clubs), and, at last, one falls backward into the mud, and the other runs away. When he comes back the dispute is settled, as the iron-bound bamboo of the loser witnesses. Yet they are not grateful to the Mugger. No, they cry 'Murder!' and their families fight with sticks, twenty a-side. My people are good people — upland Jats — Malwais of the

Bet. They do not give blows for sport, and, when the fight is done, the old Mugger waits far down the river, out of sight of the village, behind the kikar-scrub yonder. Then come they down, my broad-shouldered Jats — eight or nine together under the stars, bearing the dead man upon a bed. They are old men with gray beards, and voices as deep as mine. They light a little fire — ah! how well I know that fire! — and they drink tobacco, and they nod their heads together forward in a ring, or sideways toward the dead man upon the bank. They say the English Law will come with a rope for this matter, and that such a man's family will be ashamed, because such a man must be hanged in the great square of the Jail. Then say the friends of the dead, 'Let him hang!' and the talk is all to do over again — once, twice, twenty times in the long night. Then says one, at last, 'The fight was a fair fight. Let us take blood-money, a little more than is offered by the slayer, and we will say no more about it.' Then do they haggle over the blood-money, for the dead was a strong man, leaving many sons. Yet before amratvela (sunrise) they put the fire to him a little, as the custom is, and the dead man comes to me, and *he* says no more about it. Aha! my children, the Mugger knows — the Mugger knows — and my Malwah Jats are a good people!"

"They are too close — too narrow in the hand for my crop," croaked the Adjutant. "They waste not the polish on the cow's horn, as the saying is; and, again, who can glean after a Malwai?"

"Ah, I — glean — *them,*" said the Mugger.

"Now, in Calcutta of the South, in the old days," the Adjutant went on, "everything was thrown into the streets, and we picked and chose. Those wore dainty seasons. But today they keep their streets as clean as the outside of an egg, and my people fly away. To be clean is one thing; to dust, sweep, and sprinkle seven times a day wearies the very Gods themselves."

"There was a down-country jackal had it from a brother, who told me, that in Calcutta of the South all the jackals were as fat as otters in the Rains," said the Jackal, his mouth watering at the bare thought of it.

"Ah, but the white-faces are there — the English, and they bring dogs from somewhere down the river in boats — big fat dogs — to keep those same jackals lean," said the Adjutant.

"They are, then, as hard-hearted as these people? I might have known. Neither earth, sky, nor water shows charity to a jackal. I saw the tents of a white-face last season, after the Rains, and I also took a new yellow bridle to eat. The white-faces do not dress their leather in the proper way. It made me very sick."

"That was better than my case," said the Adjutant. "When I was in my third season, a young and a bold bird, I went down to the river where the big boats come in. The boats of the English are thrice as big as this village."

"He has been as far as Delhi, and says all the people there walk on their heads," muttered the Jackal. The Mugger opened his left eye, and looked keenly at the Adjutant.

"It is true," the big bird insisted. "A liar only lies when he hopes to be believed. No one who had not seen those boats *could* believe this truth."

"*That* is more reasonable," said the Mugger. "And then?"

"From the insides of this boat they were taking out great pieces of white stuff, which, in a little while, turned to water. Much split off, and fell about on the shore, and the rest they swiftly put into a house with thick walls. But a boatman, who laughed, took a piece no larger than a small dog, and threw it to me. I — all my people — swallow without reflection, and that piece

I swallowed as is our custom. Immediately I was afflicted with an excessive cold which, beginning in my crop, ran down to the extreme end of my toes, and deprived me even of speech, while the boatmen laughed at me. Never have I felt such cold. I danced in my grief and amazement till I could recover my breath and then I danced and cried out against the falseness of this world; and the boatmen derided me till they fell down. The chief wonder of the matter, setting aside that marvelous coldness, was that there was nothing at all in my crop when I had finished my lamentings!"

The Adjutant had done his very best to describe his feelings after swallowing a seven-pound lump of Wenham Lake ice, off an American ice-ship, in the days before Calcutta made her ice by machinery; but as he did not know what ice was, and as the Mugger and the Jackal knew rather less, the tale missed fire.

"Anything," said the Mugger, shutting his left eye again — "*anything* is possible that comes out of a boat thrice the size of Mugger-Ghaut. My village is not a small one."

There was a whistle overhead on the bridge, and the Delhi Mail slid across, all the carriages gleaming with light, and the shadows faithfully following along the river. It clanked away into the dark again; but the Mugger and the Jackal were so well used to it that they never turned their heads.

"Is that anything less wonderful than a boat thrice the size of Mugger-Ghaut?" said the bird, looking up.

"I saw that built, child. Stone by stone I saw the bridge-piers rise, and when the men fell off (they were wondrous sure-footed for the most part — but *when* they fell) I was ready. After the first pier was made they never thought to look down the stream for the body to burn. There, again, I saved much trouble. There was nothing strange in the building of the bridge," said the Mugger.

"But that which goes across, pulling the roofed carts! That is strange," the Adjutant repeated. "It is, past any doubt, a new breed of bullock. Some day it will not be able to keep its foothold up yonder, and will fall as the men did. The old Mugger will then be ready."

The Jackal looked at the Adjutant and the Adjutant looked at the Jackal. If there was one thing they were more certain of than another, it was that the engine was everything in the wide world except a bullock. The Jackal had watched it time and again from the aloe hedges by the side of the line, and the Adjutant had seen engines since the first locomotive ran in India. But the Mugger had only looked up at the thing from below, where the brass dome seemed rather like a bullock's hump.

"M — yes, a new kind of bullock," the Mugger repeated ponderously, to make himself quite sure in his own mind; and "Certainly it is a bullock," said the Jackal.

"And again it might be —" began the Mugger pettishly.

"Certainly — most certainly," said the Jackal, without waiting for the other to finish.

"What?" said the Mugger angrily, for he could feel that the others knew more than he did. "What might it be? *I* never finished my words. You said it was a bullock."

"It is anything the Protector of the Poor pleases. I am *his* servant — not the servant of the thing that crosses the river."

"Whatever it is, it is white-face work," said the Adjutant; "and for my own part, I would not lie out upon a place so near to it as this bar."

"You do not know the English as I do," said the

Mugger. "There was a white-face here when the bridge was built, and he would take a boat in the evenings and shuffle with his feet on the bottom-boards, and whisper: 'Is he here? Is he there? Bring me my gun.' I could hear him before I could see him — each sound that he made — creaking and puffing and rattling his gun, up and down the river. As surely as I had picked up one of his workmen, and thus saved great expense in wood for the burning, so surely would he come down to the Ghaut, and shout in a loud voice that he would hunt me, and rid the river of me — the Mugger of Mugger-Ghaut! *Me!* Children, I have swum under the bottom of his boat for hour after hour, and heard him fire his gun at logs; and when I was well sure he was wearied, I have risen by his side and snapped my jaws in his face. When the bridge was finished he went away. All the English hunt in that fashion, except when they are hunted."

"Who hunts the white-faces?" yapped the Jackal excitedly.

"No one now, but I have hunted them in my time."

"I remember a little of that Hunting. I was young then," said the Adjutant, clattering his beak significantly.

"I was well established here. My village was being builded for the third time, as I remember, when my cousin, the Gavial, brought me word of rich waters above Benares. At first I would not go, for my cousin, who is a fish-eater, does not always know the good from the bad; but I heard my people talking in the evenings, and what they said made me certain."

"And what did they say?" the Jackal asked.

"They said enough to make me, the Mugger of Mugger-Ghaut, leave water and take to my feet. I went by night, using the littlest streams as they served me; but it was the beginning of the hot weather, and all streams were low. I crossed dusty roads; I went through tall grass; I climbed hills in the moonlight. Even rocks did I climb, children — consider this well. I crossed the tail of Sirhind, the waterless, before I could find the set of the little rivers that flow Gungaward. I was a month's journey from my own people and the river that I knew. That was very marvelous!"

"What food on the way?" said the Jackal, who kept his soul in his little stomach, and was not a bit impressed by the Mugger's land travels.

"That which I could find — *cousin*," said the Mugger slowly, dragging each word.

Now you do not call a man a cousin in India unless you think you can establish some kind of blood-relationship, and as it is only in old fairy-tales that the Mugger ever marries a jackal, the Jackal knew for what reason he had been suddenly lifted into the Mugger's family circle. If they had been alone he would not have cared, but the Adjutant's eyes twinkled with mirth at the ugly jest.

"Assuredly, Father, I might have known," said the Jackal. A mugger does not care to be called a father of jackals, and the Mugger of Mugger-Ghaut said as much — and a great deal more which there is no use in repeating here.

"The Protector of the Poor has claimed kinship. How can I remember the precise degree? Moreover, we eat the same food. He has said it," was the Jackal's reply.

That made matters rather worse, for what the Jackal hinted at was that the Mugger must have eaten his food on that land-march fresh and fresh every day, instead of keeping it by him till it was in a fit and proper condition, as every self-respecting mugger and most wild beasts do when they can. Indeed, one of the worst terms of contempt along the River-bed is "eater of fresh meat." It is nearly as bad as calling a man a cannibal.

"That food was eaten thirty seasons ago," said the Adjutant quietly. "If we talk for thirty seasons more it will never come back. Tell us, now, what happened when the good waters were reached after thy most wonderful land journey. If we listened to the howling of every jackal the business of the town would stop, as the saying is."

The Mugger must have been grateful for the interruption, because he went on, with a rush:

"By the Right and Left of Gunga! when I came there never did I see such waters!"

"Were they better, then, than the big flood of last season?" said the Jackal.

"Better! That flood was no more than comes every five years — a handful of drowned strangers, some chickens, and a dead bullock in muddy water with cross-currents. But the season I think of, the river was low, smooth, and even, and, as the Gavial had warned me, the dead English came down, touching each other. I got my girth in that season — my girth and my depth. From Agra, by Etawah and the broad waters by Allahabad —"

"Oh, the eddy that set under the walls of the fort at Allahabad!" said the Adjutant. "They came in there like widgeon to the reeds, and round and round they swung — thus!"

He went off into his horrible dance again, while the Jackal looked on enviously. He naturally could not remember the terrible year of the Mutiny they were talking about. The Mugger continued:

"Yes, by Allahabad one lay still in the slack-water and let twenty go by to pick one; and, above all, the English were not cumbered with jewelry and nose-rings and anklets as my women are nowadays. To delight in ornaments is to end with a rope for a necklace, as the saying is. All the muggers of all the rivers grew fat then, but it was my Fate to be fatter than them all. The news was that the English were being hunted into the rivers, and by the Right and Left of Gunga! we believed it was true. So far as I went south I believed it to he true; and I went down-stream beyond Monghyr and the tombs that look over the river."

"I know that place," said the Adjutant. "Since those days Monghyr is a lost city. Very few live there now."

"Thereafter I worked up-stream very slowly and lazily, and a little above Monghyr there came down a boatful of white-faces — alive! They were, as I remember, women, lying under a cloth spread over sticks, and crying aloud. There was never a gun fired at us, the watchers of the fords in those days. All the guns were busy elsewhere. We could hear them day and night inland, coming and going as the wind shifted. I rose up full before the boat, because I had never seen white-faces alive, though I knew them well — otherwise. A naked white child kneeled by the side of the boat, and, stooping over, must needs try to trail his hands in the river. It is a pretty thing to see how a child loves running water. I had fed that day, but there was yet a little unfilled space within me. Still, it was for sport and not for food that I rose at the child's hands. They were so clear a mark that I did not even look when I closed; but they were so small that though my jaws rang true — I am sure of that — the child drew them up swiftly, unhurt. They must have passed between tooth and tooth — those small white hands. I should have caught him cross-wise at the elbows; but, as I said, it was only for sport and desire to see new things that I rose at all. They cried out one after another in the boat, and presently I rose again to watch them. The boat was too heavy to push over. They were only women, but he who trusts a woman will walk on duckweed in a pool, as the saying is: and by the Right and Left of Gunga, that is truth!"

"Once a woman gave me some dried skin from a fish," said the Jackal. "I had hoped to get her baby, but horse-food is better than the kick of a horse, as the saying is. What did thy woman do?"

"She fired at me with a short gun of a kind I have never seen before or since. Five times, one after another" (the Mugger must have met with an old-fashioned revolver); "and I stayed open-mouthed and gaping, my head in the smoke. Never did I see such a thing. Five times, as swiftly as I wave my tail — thus!"

The Jackal, who had been growing more and more interested in the story, had just time to leap back as the huge tail swung by like a scythe.

"Not before the fifth shot," said the Mugger, as though he had never dreamed of stunning one of his listeners — " not before the fifth shot did I sink, and I rose in time to hear a boatman telling all those white women that I was most certainly dead. One bullet had gone under a neck-plate of mine. I know not if it is there still, for the reason I cannot turn my head. Look and see, child. It will show that my tale is true."

"I?" said the Jackal. "Shall an eater of old shoes, a bone-cracker, presume, to doubt the word of the Envy of the River? May my tail be bitten off by blind puppies if the shadow of such a thought has crossed my humble mind! The Protector of the Poor has condescended to inform me, his slave, that once in his life he has been wounded by a woman. That is sufficient, and I will tell the tale to all my children, asking for no proof."

"Overmuch civility is sometimes no better than overmuch discourtesy, for, as the saying is, one can choke a guest with curds. I do *not* desire that any children of thine should know that the Mugger of Mugger-Ghaut took his only wound from a woman. They will have much else to think of if they get their meat as miserably as does their father."

"It is forgotten long ago! It was never said! There never was a white woman! There was no boat! Nothing whatever happened at all."

The Jackal waved his brush to show how completely everything was wiped out of his memory, and sat down with an air.

"Indeed, very many things happened," said the Mugger, beaten in his second attempt that night to get the better of his friend. (Neither bore malice, however. Eat and be eaten was fair law along the river, and the Jackal came in for his share of plunder when the Mugger had finished a meal.) "I left that boat and went up-stream, and, when I had reached Arrah and the back-waters behind it, there were no more dead English. The river was empty for a while. Then came one or two dead, in red coats, not English, but of one kind all — Hindus and Purbeeahs — then five and six abreast, and at last, from Arrah to the North beyond Agra, it was as though whole villages had walked into the water. They came out of little creeks one after another, as the logs come down in the Rains. When the river rose they rose also in companies from the shoals they had rested upon; and the falling flood dragged them with it across the fields and through the Jungle by the long hair. All night, too, going North, I heard the guns, and by day the shod feet of men crossing fords, and that noise which a heavy cart-wheel makes on sand under water; and every ripple brought more dead. At last even I was afraid, for I said: 'If this thing happen to men, how shall the Mugger of Mugger-Ghaut escape?' There were boats, too, that came up behind me without sails, burning continually, as the cotton-boats sometimes burn, but never sinking."

"Ah!" said the Adjutant. "Boats like those come to Calcutta of the South. They are tall and black, they beat up the water behind them with a tail, and they —"

"Are thrice as big as my village. *My* boats were low and white; they beat up the water on either side of them and were no larger than the boats of one who speaks truth should be. They made me very afraid, and I left water and went back to this my river, hiding by day and walking by night, when I could not find little streams to help me. I came to my village again, but I did not hope to see any of my people there. Yet they were ploughing and sowing and reaping, and going to and fro in their fields, as quietly as their own cattle."

"Was there still good food in the river?" said the Jackal.

"More than I had any desire for. Even I — and I do not eat mud — even I was tired, and, as I remember, a little frightened of this constant coming down of the silent ones. I heard my people say in my village that all the English were dead; but those that came, face down, with the current were *not* English, as my people saw. Then my people said that it was best to say nothing at all, but to pay the tax and plough the land. After a long time the river cleared, and those that came down it had been clearly drowned by the floods, as I could well see; and though it was not so easy then to get food, I was heartily glad of it. A little killing here and there is no bad thing — but even the Mugger is sometimes satisfied, as the saying is."

"Marvelous! Most truly marvelous!" said the Jackal. "I am become fat through merely hearing about so much good eating. And afterward what, if it be permitted to ask, did the Protector of the Poor do?"

"I said to myself — and by the Right and Left of Gunga! I locked my jaws on that vow — I said I would never go roving anymore. So I lived by the Ghaut, very close to my own people, and I watched over them year after year; and they loved me so much that they threw marigold wreaths at my head whenever they saw it lift. Yes, and my Fate has been very kind to me, and the river is good enough to respect my poor and infirm presence; only —"

"No one is all happy from his beak to his tail," said the Adjutant sympathetically. "What does the Mugger of Mugger-Ghaut need more?"

"That little white child which I did not get," said the Mugger, with a deep sigh. "He was very small, but I have not forgotten. I am old now, but before I die it is my desire to try one new thing. It is true they are a heavy-footed, noisy, and foolish people, and the sport would be small, but I remember the old days above Benares, and, if the child lives, he will remember still. It may be he goes up and down the bank of some river, telling how he once passed his hands between the teeth of the Mugger of Mugger-Ghaut, and lived to make a tale of it. My Fate has been very kind, but that plagues me sometimes in my dreams — the thought of the little white child in the bows of that boat." He yawned, and closed his jaws. "And now I will rest and think. Keep silent, my children, and respect the aged."

He turned stiffly, and shuffled to the top of the sand-bar, while the Jackal drew back with the Adjutant to the shelter of a tree stranded on the end nearest the railway bridge.

"That was a pleasant and profitable life," he grinned, looking up inquiringly at the bird who towered above him. "And not once, mark you, did he think fit to tell me where a morsel might have been left along the banks. Yet I have told *him* a hundred times of good things wallowing down-stream. How true is the saying, 'All the world forgets the Jackal and the Barber when the news has been told!' Now he is going to sleep! Arrh!"

"How can a jackal hunt with a Mugger?" said the

Adjutant coolly. "Big thief and little thief; it is easy to say who gets the pickings."

The Jackal turned, whining impatiently, and was going to curl himself up under the tree-trunk, when suddenly he cowered, and looked up through the draggled branches at the bridge almost above his head.

"What now?" said the Adjutant, opening his wings uneasily.

"Wait till we see. The wind blows from us to them, but they are not looking for us — those two men."

"Men, is it? My office protects me. All India knows I am holy." The Adjutant, being a first-class scavenger, is allowed to go where he pleases, and so this one never flinched.

"I am not worth a blow from anything better than an old shoe," said the Jackal, and listened again. "Hark to that footfall!" he went on. "That was no country leather, but the shod foot of a white-face. Listen again! Iron hits iron up there! It is a gun! Friend, those heavy-footed, foolish English are coming to speak with the Mugger."

"Warn him, then. He was called Protector of the Poor by some one not unlike a starving Jackal but a little time ago."

"Let my cousin protect his own hide. He has told me again and again there is nothing to fear from the white-faces. They must be white-faces. Not a villager of Mugger-Ghaut would dare to come after him. See, I said it was a gun! Now, with good luck, we shall feed before daylight. He cannot hear well out of water, and — this time it is not a woman!"

A shiny barrel glittered for a minute in the moonlight on the girders. The Mugger was lying on the sand-bar as still as his own shadow, his fore-feet spread out a little, his head dropped between them, snoring like a — mugger.

A voice on the bridge whispered: "It's an odd shot — straight down almost — but as safe as houses. Better try behind the neck. Golly! what a brute! The villagers will be wild if he's shot, though. He's the deota [godling] of these parts."

"Don't care a rap," another voice answered; "he took about fifteen of my best coolies while the bridge was building, and it's time he was put a stop to. I've been after him in a boat for weeks. Stand by with the Martini as soon as I've given him both barrels of this."

"Mind the kick, then. A double four-bore's no joke."

"That's for him to decide. Here goes!"

There was a roar like the sound of a small cannon (the biggest sort of elephant-rifle is not very different from some artillery), and a double streak of flame, followed by the stinging crack of a Martini, whose long bullet makes nothing of a crocodile's plates. But the explosive bullets did the work. One of them struck just behind the Mugger's neck, a hand's-breadth to the left of thle backbone, while the other burst a little lower down, at the beginning of the tail. In ninety-nine cases out of a hundred a mortally-wounded crocodile can scramble to deep water and get away; but the Mugger of Mugger-Ghaut was literally broken into three pieces. He hardly moved his head before the life went out of him, and he lay as flat as the Jackal.

"Thunder and lightning! Lightning and thunder!" said that miserable little beast. "Has the thing that pulls the covered carts over the bridge tumbled at last?"

"It is no more than a gun," said the Adjutant, though his very tail-feathers quivered. "Nothing more than a gun. He is certainly dead. Here come the white-faces."

The two Englishmen had hurried down from the bridge and across to the sand-bar, where they stood admiring the length of the Mugger. Then a native with an axe cut off the big head, and four men dragged it across the spit.

"The last time that I had my hand in a Mugger's mouth," said one of the Englishmen, stooping down (he was the man who had built the bridge), "it was when I was about five years old — coming down the river by boat to Monghyr. I was a Mutiny baby, as they call it. Poor mother was in the boat, too, and she often told me how she fired dad's old pistol at the beast's head."

"Well, you've certainly had your revenge on the chief of the clan — even if the gun has made your nose bleed. Hi, you boatmen! Haul that head up the bank, and we'll boil it for the skull. The skin's too knocked about to keep. Come along to bed now. This was worth sitting up all night for, wasn't it?"

*C*uriously enough, the Jackal and the Adjutant made the very same remark not three minutes after the men had left.

A Ripple Song

Once a ripple came to land
  In the golden sunset burning —
Lapped against a maiden's hand,
  By the ford returning.

Dainty foot and gentle breast —
  Here, across, be glad and rest.
"Maiden, wait," the ripple saith.
  "Wait awhile, for I am Death!"

"Where my lover calls I go —
  Shame it were to treat him coldly —
'Twas a fish that circled so,
  Turning over boldly."

Dainty foot and tender heart,
  Wait the loaded ferry-cart.
"Wait, ah, wait!" the ripple saith;
  "Maiden, wait, for I am Death!"

"When my lover calls I haste —
  Dame Disdain was never wedded!"

Ripple-ripple round her waist,
  Clear the current eddied.

Foolish heart and faithful hand,
  Little feet that touched no land.
Far away the ripple sped,
  Ripple — ripple — running red!

The King's Ankus

These are the Four that are never content, that have
        never been filled since the Dews began —
Jacala's mouth, and the glut of the Kite, and the
        hands of the Ape, and the Eyes of Man.
                                    Jungle Saying

*K*aa, the big Rock Python, had changed his skin
for perhaps the two-hundredth time since his birth;
and Mowgli, who never forgot that he owed his life to
Kaa for a night's work at Cold Lairs, which you may
perhaps remember, went to congratulate him. Skin-
changing always makes a snake moody and depressed
till the new skin begins to shine and look beautiful.
Kaa never made fun of Mowgli anymore, but accepted
him, as the other Jungle People did, for the Master of
the Jungle, and brought him all the news that a python
of his size would naturally hear. What Kaa did not
know about the Middle Jungle, as they call it, — the
life that runs close to the earth or under it, the boulder,
burrow, and the tree-bole life, — might have been
written upon the smallest of his scales.

That afternoon Mowgli was sitting in the circle of

Kaa!s great coils, fingering the flaked and broken old skin that lay all looped and twisted among the rocks just as Kaa had left it. Kaa had very courteously packed himself under Mowgli's broad, bare shoulders, so that the boy was really resting in a living armchair.

"Even to the scales of the eyes it is perfect," said Mowgli, under his breath, playing with the old skin. "Strange to see the covering of one's own head at one's own feet!"

"Aye, but I lack feet," said Kaa; "and since this is the custom of all my people, I do not find it strange. Does thy skin never feel old and harsh?"

"Then go I and wash, Flathead; but, it is true, in the great heats I have wished I could slough my skin without pain, and run skinless."

"I wash, and *also* I take off my skin. How looks the new coat?"

Mowgli ran his hand down the diagonal checkerings of the immense back. "The Turtle is harder-backed, but not so gay," he said judgmatically. "The Frog, my name-bearer, is more gay, but not so hard. It is very beautiful to see — like the mottling in the mouth of a lily."

"It needs water. A new skin never comes to full color before the first bath. Let us go bathe."

"I will carry thee," said Mowgli; and he stooped down, laughing, to lift the middle section of Kaa's great body, just where the barrel was thickest. A man might just, as well have tried to heave up a two-foot water-main; and Kaa lay still, puffing with quiet amusement. Then the regular evening game began — the Boy in the flush of his great strength, and the Python in his sumptuous new skin, standing up one against the other for a wrestling match — a trial of eye and strength. Of course, Kaa could have crushed a dozen Mowglis if he had let himself go; but he played carefully, and never loosed one-tenth of his power. Ever since Mowgli was strong enough to endure a little rough handling, Kaa had taught him this game, and it suppled his limbs as nothing else could. Sometimes Mowgli would stand lapped almost to his throat in Kaa's shifting coils, striving to get one arm free and catch him by the throat. Then Kaa would give way limply, and Mowgli, with both quick-moving feet, would try to cramp the purchase of that huge tail as it flung backward feeling for a rock or a stump. They would rock to and fro, head to head, each waiting for his chance, till the beautiful, statuelike group melted in a whirl of black-and-yellow coils and struggling legs and arms, to rise up again and again. "Now! now! now!" said Kaa, making feints with his head that even Mowgli's quick hand could not turn aside. "Look! I touch thee here, Little Brother! Here, and here! Are thy hands numb? Here again!"

The game always ended in one way — with a straight, driving blow of the head that knocked the boy over and over. Mowgli could never learn the guard for that lightning lunge, and, as Kaa said, there was not the least use in trying.

"Good hunting!" Kaa grunted at last; and Mowgli, as usual, was shot away half a dozen yards, gasping and laughing. He rose with his fingers full of grass, and followed Kaa to the wise snake's pet bathing-place — a deep, pitchy-black pool surrounded with rocks, and made interesting by sunken tree-stumps. The boy slipped in, Jungle-fashion, without a sound, and dived across; rose, too, without a sound, and turned on his back, his arms behind his head, watching the moon rising above the rocks, and breaking up her reflection in the water with his toes. Kaa's diamond-shaped head cut the pool like a razor, and came out to rest on Mowgli's shoulder. They lay still, soaking luxuriously in the cool water.

"It is *very* good," said Mowgli at last, sleepily. "Now, in the Man-Pack, at this hour, as I remember, they laid them down upon hard pieces of wood in the inside of a mud-trap, and, having carefully shut out all the clean winds, drew foul cloth over their heavy heads and made evil songs through their noses. It is better in the Jungle."

A hurrying cobra slipped down over a rock and drank, gave them "Good hunting!" and went away.

"Sssh!" said Kaa, as though he had suddenly remembered something. "So the Jungle gives thee all that thou hast ever desired, Little Brother?"

"Not all," said Mowgli, laughing; "else there would be a new and strong Shere Khan to kill once a moon. Now, I could kill with my own hands, asking no help of buffaloes. And also I have wished the sun to shine in the middle of the Rains, and the Rains to cover the sun in the deep of summer; and also I have never gone empty but I wished that I had killed a goat; and also I have never killed a goat but I wished it had been buck; nor buck but I wished it had been nilghai. But thus do we feel, all of us."

"Thou hast no other desire?" the big snake demanded.

"What more can I wish? I have the Jungle, and the favor of the Jungle! Is there more anywhere between sunrise and sunset?"

"Now, the Cobra said —" Kaa began. "What cobra? He that went away just now said nothing. He was hunting."

"It was another."

"Hast thou many dealings with the Poison People? I give them their own path. They carry death in the fore-tooth, and that is not good — for they are so small. But what hood is this thou hast spoken with?"

Kaa rolled slowly in the water like a steamer in a

beam sea. "Three or four moons since," said he, "I hunted in Cold Lairs, which place thou hast not forgotten. And the thing I hunted fled shrieking past the tanks and to that house whose side I once broke for thy sake, and ran into the ground."

"But the people of Cold Lairs do not live in burrows." Mowgli knew that Kaa was telling of the Monkey People.

"This thing was not living, but seeking to live," Kaa replied, with a quiver of his tongue. "He ran into a burrow that led very far. I followed, and having killed, I slept. When I waked I went forward."

"Under the earth?"

"Even so, coming at last upon a White Hood [a white cobra], who spoke of things beyond my knowledge, and showed me many things I had never before seen."

"New game? Was it good hunting?" Mowgli turned quickly on his side.

"It was no game, and would have broken all my teeth; but the White Hood said that a man — he spoke as one that knew the breed — that a man would give the breath under his ribs for only the sight of those things."

"We will look," said Mowgli. "I now remember that I was once a man."

"Slowly — slowly. It was haste killed the Yellow Snake that ate the sun. We two spoke together under the earth, and I spoke of thee, naming thee as a man. Said the White Hood (and he is indeed as old as the Jungle): 'It is long since I have seen a man. Let him come, and he shall see all these things, for the least of which very many men would die.'"

"That *must* be new game. And yet the Poison People do not tell us when game is afoot. They are an unfriendly folk."

"It is *not* game. It is — it is — I cannot say what it is."

"We will go there. I have never seen a White Hood,

and I wish to see the other things. Did he kill them?"

"They are all dead things. He says he is the keeper of them all."

"Ah! As a wolf stands above meat he has taken to his own lair. Let us go."

Mowgli swam to bank, rolled on the grass to dry himself, and the two set off for Cold Lairs, the deserted city of which you may have heard. Mowgli was not the least afraid of the Monkey People in those days, but the Monkey People had the liveliest horror of Mowgli. Their tribes, however, were raiding in the Jungle, and so Cold Lairs stood empty and silent in the moonlight. Kaa led up to the ruins of the queens' pavilion that stood on the terrace, slipped over the rubbish, and dived down the half-choked staircase that went underground from the center of the pavilion. Mowgli gave the snake-call, — "We be of one blood, ye and I," — and followed on his hands and knees. They crawled a long distance down a sloping passage that turned and twisted several times, and at last came to where the root of some great tree, growing thirty feet overhead, had forced out a solid stone in the wall. They crept through the gap, and found themselves in a large vault, whose domed roof had been also broken away by tree-roots so that a few streaks of light dropped down into the darkness.

"A safe lair," said Mowgli, rising to his firm feet, "but overfar to visit daily. And now what do we see?"

"Am I nothing?" said a voice in the middle of the vault; and Mowgli saw something white move till, little by little, there stood up the hugest cobra he had ever set eyes on — a creature nearly eight feet long, and bleached by being in darkness to an old ivory-white. Even the spectacle-marks of his spread hood had faded to faint yellow. His eyes were as red as rubies, and altogether he was most wonderful.

"Good hunting!" said Mowgli, who carried his manners with his knife, and that never left him.

"What of the city?" said the White Cobra, without answering the greeting. "What of the great, the walled city — the city of a hundred elephants and twenty thousand horses, and cattle past counting — the city of the King of Twenty Kings? I grow deaf here, and it is long since I heard their war-gongs."

"The Jungle is above our heads," said Mowgli. "I know only Hathi and his sons among elephants. Bagheera has slain all the horses in one village, and — what is a King?"

"I told thee," said Kaa softly to the Cobra, — "I told thee, four moons ago, that thy city was not."

"The city — the great city of the forest whose gates are guarded by the King's towers — can never pass. They builded it before my father's father came from the egg, and it shall endure when my son's sons are as white as I! Salomdhi, son of Chandrabija, son of Viyeja, son of Yegasuri, made it in the days of Bappa Rawal. Whose cattle are *ye*?"

"It is a lost trail," said Mowgli, turning to Kaa. "I know not his talk."

"Nor I. He is very old. Father of Cobras, there is only the Jungle here, as it has been since the beginning."

"Then who is *he*," said the White Cobra, "sitting down before me, unafraid, knowing not the name of the King, talking our talk through a man's lips? Who is he with the knife and the snake's tongue?"

"Mowgli they call me," was the answer. "I am of the Jungle. The wolves are my people, and Kaa here is my brother. Father of Cobras, who art thou?"

"I am the Warden of the King's Treasure. Kurrun Raja built the stone above me, in the days when my skin was dark, that I might teach death to those who came to steal. Then they let down the treasure through the stone, and I heard the song of the Brahmins my masters."

"Umm!" said Mowgli to himself. "I have dealt with one Brahmin already, in the Man-Pack, and — I know what I know. Evil comes here in a little."

"Five times since I came here has the stone been lifted, but always to let down more, and never to take away. There are no riches like these riches — the treasures of a hundred kings. But it is long and long since the stone was last moved, and I think that my city has forgotten."

"There is no city. Look up. Yonder are roots of the great trees tearing the stones apart. Trees and men do not grow together," Kaa insisted.

"Twice and thrice have men found their way here," the White Cobra answered savagely; "but they never spoke till I came upon them groping in the dark, and then they cried only a little time. But ye come with lies, Man and Snake both, and would have me believe the city is not, and that my wardship ends. Little do men change in the years. But I change never! Till the stone is lifted, and the Brahmins come down singing the songs that I know, and feed me with warm milk, and take me to the light again, I — I — *I*, and no other, am the Warden of the King's Treasure! The city is dead, ye say, and here are the roots of the trees? Stoop down, then, and take what ye will. Earth has no treasure like to these. Man with the snake's tongue, if thou canst go alive by the way that thou hast entered it, the lesser Kings will be thy servants!"

"Again the trail is lost," said Mowgli coolly. "Can any jackal have burrowed so deep and bitten this great White Hood? He is surely mad. Father of Cobras, I see nothing here to take away."

"By the Gods of the Sun and Moon, it is the madness of death upon the boy!" hissed the Cobra. "Before thine eyes close I will allow thee this favor. Look thou, and see what man has never seen before!"

"They do not well in the Jungle who speak to Mowgli of favors," said the boy, between his teeth; "but the dark changes all, as I know. I will look, if that please thee."

He stared with puckered-up eyes round the vault, and then lifted up from the floor a handful of something that glittered.

"Oho!" said he, "this is like the stuff they play with in the Man-Pack: only this is yellow and the other was brown."

He let the gold pieces fall, and move forward. The floor of the vault was buried some five or six feet deep in coined gold and silver that had burst from the sacks it had been originally stored in, and, in the long years, the metal had packed and settled as sand packs at low tide. On it and in it and rising through it, as wrecks lift through the sand, were jeweled elephant-howdahs of embossed silver, studded with plates of hammered gold, and adorned with carbuncles and turquoises. There were palanquins and litters for carrying queens, framed and braced with silver and enamel, with jade-handled poles and amber curtain-rings; there were golden candlesticks hung with pierced emeralds that quivered on the branches; there were studded images, five feet high, of forgotten gods, silver with jeweled eyes; there were coats of mail, gold inlaid on steel, and fringed with rotted and blackened seed-pearls; there were helmets, crested and beaded with pigeon's-blood rubies; there were shields of lacquer, of tortoise-shell and rhinoceros-hide, strapped and bossed with red gold and set with emeralds at the edge; there were sheaves of diamond-hilted swords, daggers, and hunting-knives; there were golden sacrificial bowls and ladles, and portable altars of a shape that never sees the light of day; there were jade cups and bracelets; there were incense-burners, combs, and pots for perfume, henna, and eye-powder, all in embossed gold; there were nose-rings, armlets, head-bands, finger-rings, and girdles past any counting; there were belts, seven fingers broad, of square-cut diamonds and rubies, and wooden boxes, trebly clamped with iron, from which the wood had fallen away in powder, showing the pile of uncut star-sapphires, opals, cat's-eyes, sapphires, rubies, diamonds, emeralds, and garnets within.

The White Cobra was right. No mere money would begin to pay the value of this treasure, the sifted pickings of centuries of war, plunder, trade, and taxation. The coins alone were priceless, leaving out of count all the precious stones; and the dead weight of the gold and silver alone might be two or three hundred tons. Every native ruler in India today, however poor, has a hoard to which he is always adding; and though, once in a long while, some enlightened prince may send off forty or fifty bullock-cart loads of silver to be exchanged for Government securities, the bulk of them keep their treasure and the knowledge of it very closely to themselves.

But Mowgli naturally did not understand what these things meant. The knives interested him a little, but they did not balance so well as his own, and so he dropped them. At last he found something really fascinating laid on the front of a howdah half buried in the coins. It was a three-foot ankus, or elephant-goad — something like a small boat-hook. The top was one round, shining ruby, and eight inches of the handle below it were studded with rough turquoises close together, giving a most satisfactory grip. Below them was a rim of jade with a flower-pattern running round it — only the leaves were emeralds, and the blossoms were rubies sunk in the cool, green stone. The rest of

the handle was a shaft of pure ivory, while the point
— the spike and hook — was gold-inlaid steel with
pictures of elephant-catching; and the pictures at-
tracted Mowgli, who saw that they had something to
do with his friend Hathi the Silent.

The White Cobra had been following him closely.

"Is this not worth dying to behold?" he said. "Have
I not done thee a great favor?"

"I do not understand," said Mowgli. "The things are
hard and cold, and by no means good to eat. But this"
— he lifted the ankus — "I desire to take away, that I
may see it in the sun. Thou sayest they are all thine?
Wilt thou give it to me, and I will bring thee frogs to
eat?"

The White Cobra fairly shook with evil delight.
"Assuredly I will give it," he said. "All that is here I will
give thee — till thou goest away."

"But I go now. This place is dark and cold, and I
wish to take the thorn-pointed thing to the Jungle."

"Look by thy foot! What is that there?" Mowgli
picked up something white and smooth. "It is the bone
of a man's head," he said quietly. "And here are two
more."

"They came to take the treasure away many years ago.
I spoke to them in the dark, and they lay still."

"But what do I need of this that is called treasure? If
thou wilt give me the ankus to take away, it is good
hunting. If not, it is good hunting nonetheless. I do
not fight with the Poison People, and I was also taught
the Master-word of thy tribe."

"There is but one Master-word here. It is mine!"

Kaa flung himself forward with blazing eyes. "Who
bade me bring the Man?" he hissed.

"I surely," the old Cobra lisped. "It is long since I
have seen Man, and this Man speaks our tongue."

"But there was no talk of killing. How can I go to

the Jungle and say that I have led him to his death?" said Kaa.

"I talk not of killing till the time. And as to thy going or not going, there is the hole in the wall. Peace, now, thou fat monkey-killer! I have but to touch thy neck, and the Jungle will know thee no longer. Never Man came here that went away with the breath under his ribs. I am the Warden of the Treasure of the King's City!"

"But, thou white worm of the dark, I tell thee there is neither king nor city! The Jungle is all about us!" cried Kaa.

"There is still the Treasure. But this can be done. Wait awhile, Kaa of the Rocks, and see the boy run. There is room for great sport here. Life is good. Run to and fro awhile, and make sport, boy!"

Mowgli put his hand on Kaa's head quietly.

"The white thing has dealt with men of the Man-Pack until now. He does not know me," he whispered. "He has asked for this hunting. Let him have it." Mowgli had been standing with the ankus held point down. He flung it from him quickly and it dropped crossways just behind the great snake's hood, pinning him to the floor. In a flash, Kaa's weight was upon the writhing body, paralyzing it from hood to tail. The red eyes burned, and the six spare inches of the head struck furiously right and left.

"Kill!" said Kaa, as Mowgli's hand went to his knife.

"No," he said, as he drew the blade; "I will never kill again save for food. But look you, Kaa!" He caught the snake behind the hood, forced the mouth open with the blade of the knife, and showed the terrible poison-fangs of the upper jaw lying black and withered in the gum. The White Cobra had outlived his poison, as a snake will.

"Thuu" ("It is dried up" – Literally, a rotted out

tree-stump), said Mowgli; and motioning Kaa away, he picked up the ankus, setting the White Cobra free.

"The King's Treasure needs a new Warden," he said gravely. "Thuu, thou hast not done well. Run to and fro and make sport, Thuu!"

"I am ashamed. Kill me!" hissed the White Cobra.

"There has been too much talk of killing. We will go now. I take the thorn-pointed thing, Thuu, because I have fought and worsted thee."

"See, then, that the thing does not kill thee at last. It is Death! Remember, it is Death! There is enough in that thing to kill the men of all my city. Not long wilt thou hold it, Jungle Man, nor he who takes it from thee. They will kill, and kill, and kill for its sake! My strength is dried up, but the ankus will do my work. It is Death! It is Death! It is Death!"

Mowgli crawled out through the hole into the passage again, and the last that he saw was the White Cobra striking furiously with his harmless fangs at the stolid golden faces of the gods that lay on the floor, and hissing, "It is Death!"

They were glad to get to the light of day once more; and when they were back in their own Jungle and Mowgli made the ankus glitter in the morning light, he was almost as pleased as though he had found a bunch of new flowers to stick in his hair.

"This is brighter than Bagheera's eyes," he said delightedly, as he twirled the ruby. "I will show it to him; but what did the Thuu mean when he talked of death?"

"I cannot say. I am sorrowful to my tail's tail that he felt not thy knife. There is always evil at Cold Lairs — above ground or below. But now I am hungry. Dost thou hunt with me this dawn?" said Kaa.

"No; Bagheera must see this thing. Good hunting!" Mowgli danced off, flourishing the great ankus, and stopping from time to time to admire it, till he came to that part of the Jungle Bagheera chiefly used, and found him drinking after a heavy kill. Mowgli told him all his adventures from beginning to end, and Bagheera sniffed at the ankus between whiles. When Mowgli came to the White Cobra's last words, the Panther purred approvingly.

"Then the White Hood spoke the thing which is?" Mowgli asked quickly.

"I was born in the King's cages at Oodeypore, and it is in my stomach that I know some little of Man. Very many men would kill thrice in a night for the sake of that one big red stone alone."

"But the stone makes it heavy to the hand. My little bright knife is better; and — see! the red stone is not good to eat. Then *why* would they kill?"

"Mowgli, go thou and sleep. Thou hast lived among men, and —"

"I remember. Men kill because they are not hunting; — for idleness and pleasure. Wake again, Bagheera. For what use was this thorn-pointed thing made?"

Bagheera half opened his eyes — he was very sleepy — with a malicious twinkle.

"It was made by men to thrust into the head of the sons of Hathi, so that the blood should pour out. I have seen the like in the street of Oodeypore, before our cages. That thing has tasted the blood of many such as Hathi."

"But why do they thrust into the heads of elephants?"

"To teach them Man's Law. Having neither claws nor teeth, men make these things — and worse."

"Always more blood when I come near, even to the things the Man-Pack have made," said Mowgli disgustedly. He was getting a little tired of the weight of the ankus. "If I had known this, I would not have taken it. First it was Messua's blood on the thongs, and now it is Hathi's. I will use it no more. Look!"

The ankus flew sparkling, and buried itself point down thirty yards away, between the trees. "So my hands are clean of Death," said Mowgli, rubbing his palms on the fresh, moist earth. "The Thuu said Death would follow me. He is old and white and mad."

"White or black, or death or life, *I* am going to sleep, Little Brother. I cannot hunt all night and howl all day, as do some folk."

Bagheera went off to a hunting-lair that he knew, about two miles off. Mowgli made an easy way for himself up a convenient tree, knotted three or four creepers together, and in less time than it takes to tell was swinging in a hammock fifty feet above ground. Though he had no positive objection to strong daylight, Mowgli followed the custom of his friends, and used it as little as he could. When he waked among the very loud-voiced peoples that live in the trees, it was twilight once more, and he had been dreaming of the beautiful pebbles he had thrown away.

"At least I will look at the thing again," he said, and slid down a creeper to the earth; but Bagheera was before him. Mowgli could hear him snuffing in the half light.

"Where is the thorn-pointed thing?" cried Mowgli.

"A man has taken it. Here is the trail."

"Now we shall see whether the Thuu spoke truth. If the pointed thing is Death, that man will die. Let us follow."

"Kill first," said Bagheera. "An empty stomach makes a careless eye. Men go very slowly, and the Jungle is wet enough to hold the lightest mark."

They killed as soon as they could, but it was nearly three hours before they finished their meat and drink and buckled down to the trail. The Jungle People know that nothing makes up for being hurried over your meals.

"Think you the pointed thing will turn in the man's hand and kill him?" Mowgli asked. "The Thuu said it was Death."

"We shall see when we find," said Bagheera, trotting with his head low. "It is single-foot" (he meant that there was only one man), "and the weight of the thing has pressed his heel far into the ground."

"Hai! This is as clear as summer lightning," Mowgli answered; and they fell into the quick, choppy trail-trot in and out through the checkers of the moonlight, following the marks of those two bare feet.

"Now he runs swiftly," said Mowgli. "The toes are spread apart." They went on over some wet ground. "Now why does he turn aside here?"

"Wait!" said Bagheera, and flung himself forward with one superb bound as far as ever he could. The first thing to do when a trail ceases to explain itself is to cast forward without leaving, your own confusing foot-marks on the ground. Bagheera turned as he landed, and faced Mowgli, crying, "Here comes another trail to meet him. It is a smaller foot, this second trail, and the toes turn inward."

Then Mowgli ran up and looked. "It is the foot of a Gond hunter," he said. "Look! Here he dragged his bow on the grass. That is why the first trail turned aside so quickly. Big Foot hid from Little Foot."

"That is true," said Bagheera. "Now, lest by crossing each other's tracks we foul the signs, let each take one trail. I am Big Foot, Little Brother, and thou art Little Foot, the Gond."

Bagheera leaped back to the original trail, leaving Mowgli stooping above the curious narrow track of the wild little man of the woods.

"Now," said Bagheera, moving step by step along the chain of footprints, "I, Big Foot, turn aside here. Now

I hide me behind a rock and stand still," not daring to shift my feet. "Cry thy trail, Little Brother."

"Now, I, Little Foot, come to the rock," said Mowgli, running up his trail. "Now, I sit down under the rock, leaning upon my right hand, and resting my bow between my toes. I wait long, for the mark of my feet is deep here."

"I also, said Bagheera, hidden behind the rock. I wait, resting the end of the thorn-pointed thing upon a stone. It slips, for here is a scratch upon the stone. Cry thy trail, Little Brother."

"One, two twigs and a big branch are broken here," said Mowgli, in an undertone. "Now, how shall I cry *that?* Ah! It is plain now. I, Little Foot, go away making noises and tramplings so that Big Foot may hear me." He moved away from the rock pace by pace among the trees, his voice rising in the distance as he approached a little cascade. "I — go — far — away — to — where — the — noise — of — falling-water — covers — my — noise; and — here — I — wait. Cry thy trail, Bagheera, Big Foot!"

The panther had been casting in every direction to see how Big Foot's trail led away from behind the rock. Then he gave tongue:

"I come from behind the rock upon my knees, dragging the thorn-pointed thing. Seeing no one, I run. I, Big Foot, run swiftly. The trail is clear. Let each follow his own. I run!"

Bagheera swept on along the clearly-marked trail, and Mowgli followed the steps of the Gond. For some time there was silence in the Jungle.

"Where art thou, Little Foot?" cried Bagheera. Mowgli's voice answered him not fifty yards to the right.

"Um!" said the Panther, with a deep cough. "The two run side by side, drawing nearer!"

They raced on another half-mile, always keeping

about the same distance, till Mowgli, whose head was not so close to the ground as Bagheera's, cried: "They have met. Good hunting — look! Here stood Little Foot, with his knee on a rock — and yonder is Big Foot indeed!"

Not ten yards in front of them, stretched across a pile of broken rocks, lay the body of a villager of the district, a long, small-feathered Gond arrow through his back and breast.

"Was the Thuu so old and so mad, Little Brother?" said Bagheera gently. "Here is one death, at least."

"Follow on. But where is the drinker of elephant's blood — the red-eyed thorn?"

"Little Foot has it — perhaps. It is single-foot again now."

The single trail of a light man who had been running quickly and bearing a burden on his left shoulder held on round a long, low spur of dried grass, where each footfall seemed, to the sharp eyes of the trackers, marked in hot iron.

Neither spoke till the trail ran up to the ashes of a campfire hidden in a ravine.

"Again!" said Bagheera, checking as though he had been turned into stone.

The body of a little wizened Gond lay with its feet in the ashes, and Bagheera looked inquiringly at Mowgli.

"That was done with a bamboo," said the boy, after one glance. "I have used such a thing among the buffaloes when I served in the Man-Pack. The Father of Cobras — I am sorrowful that I made a jest of him — knew the breed well, as I might have known. Said I not that men kill for idleness?"

"Indeed, they killed for the sake of the red and blue stones," Bagheera answered. "Remember, I was in the King's cages at Oodeypore."

"One, two, three, four tracks," said Mowgli, stooping over the ashes. "Four tracks of men with shod feet. They do not go so quickly as Gonds. Now, what evil had the little woodman done to them? See, they talked together, all five, standing up, before they killed him. Bagheera, let us go back. My stomach is heavy in me, and yet it heaves up and down like an oriole's nest at the end of a branch."

"It is not good hunting to leave game afoot. Follow!" said the panther. "Those eight shod feet have not gone far."

No more was said for fully an hour, as they worked up the broad trail of the four men with shod feet.

It was clear, hot daylight now, and Bagheera said, "I smell smoke."

Men are always more ready to eat than to run, Mowgli answered, trotting in and out between the low scrub bushes of the new Jungle they were exploring. Bagheera, a little to his left, made an indescribable noise in his throat.

"Here is one that has done with feeding," said he. A tumbled bundle of gay-colored clothes lay under a bush, and round it was some spilt flour.

"That was done by the bamboo again," said Mowgli. " See! that white dust is what men eat. They have taken the kill from this one, — he carried their food, — and given him for a kill to Chil, the Kite."

"It is the third," said Bagheera.

"I will go with new, big frogs to the Father of Cobras, and feed him fat," said Mowgli to himself. "The drinker of elephant's blood is Death himself — but still I do not understand!"

"Follow!" said Bagheera.

They had not gone half a mile farther when they heard Ko, the Crow, singing the death-song in the top of a tamarisk under whose shade three men were lying.

A half-dead fire smoked in the center of the circle, under an iron plate which held a blackened and burned cake of unleavened bread. Close to the fire, and blazing in the sunshine, lay the ruby-and-turquoise ankus.

"The thing works quickly; all ends here," said Bagheera. "How did *these* die, Mowgli? There is no mark on any."

A Jungle-dweller gets to learn by experience as much as many doctors know of poisonous plants and berries. Mowgli sniffed the smoke that came up from the fire, broke off a morsel of the blackened bread, tasted it, and spat it out again.

"Apple of Death," he coughed. "The first must have made it ready in the food for *these*, who killed him, having first killed the Gond."

"Good hunting, indeed! The kills follow close," said Bagheera.

"Apple of Death" is what the Jungle call thorn-apple or dhatura, the readiest poison in all India.

"What now?" said the panther. "Must thou and I kill each other for yonder red-eyed slayer?"

"Can it speak?" said Mowgli in a whisper. "Did I do it a wrong when I threw it away? Between us two it can do no wrong, for we do not desire what men desire. If it be left here, it will assuredly continue to kill men one after another as fast as nuts fall in a high wind. I have no love to men, but even I would not have them die six in a night."

"What matter? They are only men. They killed one another, and were well pleased," said Bagheera. "That first little woodman hunted well."

"They are cubs nonetheless; and a cub will drown himself to bite the moon's light on the water. The fault was mine," said Mowgli, who spoke as though he knew all about everything. "I will never again bring into the Jungle strange things — not though they be as beautiful as flowers. This" — he handled the ankus gingerly — "goes back to the Father of Cobras. But first we must sleep, and we cannot sleep near these sleepers. Also we must bury *him*, lest he run away and kill another six. Dig me a hole under that tree."

"But, Little Brother," said Bagheera, moving off to the spot, "I tell thee it is no fault of the blood-drinker. The trouble is with the men."

"All one," said Mowgli. "Dig the hole deep. When we wake I will take him up and carry him back."

*T*wo nights later, as the White Cobra sat mourning in the darkness of the vault, ashamed, and robbed, and alone, the turquoise ankus whirled through the hole in the wall, and clashed on the floor of golden coins.

"Father of Cobras," said Mowgli (he was careful to keep the other side of the wall), "get thee a young and ripe one of thine own people to help thee guard the King's Treasure, so that no man may come away alive anymore."

"Ah-ha! It returns, then. I said the thing was Death. How comes it that thou art still alive?" the old Cobra mumbled, twining lovingly round the ankus-haft.

"By the Bull that bought me, I do not know! That thing has killed six times in a night. Let him go out no more."

The Song of the Little Hunter

Ere Mor the Peacock flutters, ere the Monkey People
  cry,
  Ere Chil the Kite swoops down a furlong sheer,
Through the Jungle very softly flits a shadow and a
  sigh —
  He is Fear, O Little Hunter, he is Fear!

Very softly down the glade runs a waiting, watching
  shade,
  And the whisper spreads and widens far and near;
And the sweat is on thy brow, for he passes even
  now —
  He is Fear, O Little Hunter, he is Fear!

Ere the moon has climbed the mountain, ere the
  rocks are ribbed with light,
  When the downward-dipping trails are dank and
  drear,
Comes a breathing hard behind thee —
  snuffle-snuffle through the night —
  It is Fear, O Little Hunter, it is Fear!

On thy knees and draw the bow; bid the shrilling
　　　arrow go;
　In the empty, mocking thicket plunge the spear;
But thy hands are loosed and weak, and the blood
　　　has left thy cheek —
　It is Fear, O Little Hunter, it is Fear!

When the heat-cloud sucks the tempest, when the
　　　slivered pine trees fall,
　When the blinding, blaring rain-squalls lash and
　　　veer;
Through the war-gongs of the thunder rings a voice
　　　more loud than all —
　It is Fear, O Little Hunter, it is Fear!

Now the spates are banked and deep; now the
　　　footless boulders leap —
　Now the lightning shows each littlest leaf-rib
　　　clear —
But thy throat is shut and dried, and thy heart
　　　against thy side
　Hammers: Fear, O Little Hunter — this is Fear!

Quiquern

The People of the Eastern Ice, they are melting like
the snow —
They beg for coffee and sugar; they go where the
white men go.
The People of the Western Ice, they learn to steal
and fight;
"They sell their furs to the trading-post: they sell
their souls to the white.
The People of the Southern Ice, they trade with the
whaler's crew;
Their women have many ribbons, but their tents are
torn and few.
But the People of the Elder Ice, beyond the white
man's ken —
Their spears are made of the narwhal-horn, and they
are the last of the Men!
                                        Translation

"*H*e has opened his eyes. Look!"

"Put him in the skin again. He will be a strong dog.
On the fourth month we will name him."

"For whom?" said Amoraq.

Kadlu's eye rolled round the skin-lined snow-house till it fell on fourteen-year-old Kotuko sitting on the sleeping-bench, making a button out of walrus ivory. "Name him for me," said Kotuko, with a grin. "I shall need him one day."

Kadlu grinned back till his eyes were almost buried in the fat of his flat cheeks, and nodded to Amoraq, while the puppy's fierce mother whined to see her baby wriggling far out of reach in the little sealskin pouch hung above the warmth of the blubber-lamp. Kotuko went on with his carving, and Kadlu threw a rolled bundle of leather dog-harnesses into a tiny little room that opened from one side of the house, slipped off his heavy deerskin hunting-suit, put it into a whale-bone-net that hung above another lamp, and dropped down on the sleeping-bench to whittle at a piece of frozen seal-meat till Amoraq, his wife, should bring the regular dinner of boiled meat and blood-soup. He had been out since early dawn at the seal-holes, eight miles away, and had come home with three big seal. Half-way down the long, low snow passage or tunnel that led to the inner door of the house you could hear snappings and yelpings, as the dogs of his sleigh-team, released from the day's work, scuffled for warm places.

When the yelpings grew too loud Kotuko lazily rolled off the sleeping-bench, and picked up a whip with an eighteen-inch handle of springy whalebone, and twenty-five feet of heavy, plaited thong. He dived into the passage, where it sounded as though all the dogs were eating him alive; but that was no more than their regular grace before meals. When he crawled out at the far end, half a dozen furry heads followed him with their eyes as he went to a sort of gallows of whale-jawbones, from which the dog's meat was hung; split off the frozen stuff in big lumps with a broad-headed spear; and stood, his whip in one hand and the meat in the other. Each beast was called by name, the weakest first, and woe betide any dog that moved out of his turn; for the tapering lash would shoot out like thonged lightning, and flick away an inch or so of hair and hide. Each beast growled, snapped, choked once over his portion, and hurried back to the protection of the passage, while the boy stood upon the snow under the blazing Northern Lights and dealt out justice. The last to be served was the big black leader of the team, who kept order when the dogs were harnessed; and to him Kotuko gave a double allowance of meat as well as an extra crack of the whip.

"Ah!" said Kotuko, coiling up the lash, "I have a little one over the lamp that will make a great many howlings. *Sarpok!* Get in!"

He crawled back over the huddled dogs, dusted the dry snow from his furs with the whalebone beater that Amoraq kept by the door, tapped the skin-lined roof of the house to shake off any icicles that might have fallen from the dome of snow above, and curled up on the bench. The dogs in the passage snored and whined in their sleep, the boy-baby in Amoraq's deep fur hood kicked and choked and gurgled, and the mother of the newly-named puppy lay at Kotuko's side, her eyes fixed on the bundle of sealskin, warm and safe above the broad yellow flame of the lamp.

And all this happened far away to the north, beyond Labrador, beyond Hudson's Strait, where the great tides heave the ice about, north of Melville Peninsula — north even of the narrow Fury and Hecla Straits — on the north shore of Baffin Land, where Bylot's Island stands above the ice of Lancaster Sound like a pudding-bowl wrong side up. North of Lancaster Sound there is little we know anything about, except North Devon and Ellesmere Land; but even there live a few scattered people, next door, as it were, to the very Pole.

Kadlu was an Inuit, — what you call an Esquimau, — and his tribe, some thirty persons all told, belonged to the Tununirmiut — "the country lying at the back of something." In the maps that desolate coast is written Navy Board Inlet, but the Inuit name is best, because the country lies at the very back of everything in the world. For nine months of the year there is only ice and snow, and gale after gale, with a cold that no one can realize who has never seen the thermometer even at zero. For six months of those nine it is dark; and that is what makes it so horrible. In the three months of the summer it only freezes every other day and every night, and then the snow begins to weep off on the southerly slopes, and a few ground-willows put out their woolly buds, a tiny stonecrop or so makes believe to blossom, beaches of fine gravel and rounded stones run down to the open sea, and polished boulders and streaked rocks lift up above the granulated snow. But all that is gone in a few weeks, and the wild winter locks down again on the land; while at sea the ice tears up and down the offing, jamming and ramming, and splitting and hitting, and pounding and grounding, till it all freezes together, ten feet thick, from the land outward to deep water.

In the winter Kadlu would follow the seal to the edge of this land-ice, and spear them as they came up to breathe at their blow-holes. The seal must have open water to live and catch fish in, and in the deep of winter the ice would sometimes run eighty miles without a break from the nearest shore. In the spring he and his people retreated from the floes to the rocky mainland, where they put up tents of skins, and snared the sea-birds, or speared the young seal basking on the beaches. Later, they would go south into Baffin Land after the reindeer, and to get their year's store of salmon from the hundreds of streams and lakes of the interior;

coming back north in September or October for the musk-ox hunting and the regular winter sealery. This traveling was done with dog-sleighs, twenty and thirty miles a day, or sometimes down the coast in big skin "woman-boats," when the dogs and the babies lay among the feet of the rowers, and the women sang songs as they glided from cape to cape over the glassy, cold waters. All the luxuries that the Tununirmiut knew came from the south — driftwood for sleigh-runners, rod-iron for harpoon-tips, steel knives, tin kettles that cooked food much better than the old soap-stone affairs, flint and steel, and even matches, as well as colored ribbons for the women's hair, little cheap mirrors, and red cloth for the edging of deerskin dress-jackets. Kadlu traded the rich, creamy, twisted narwhal horn and musk-ox teeth (these are just as valuable as pearls) to the Southern Inuit, and they, in turn, traded with the whalers and the missionary-posts of Exeter and Cumberland Sounds; and so the chain went on, till a kettle picked up by a ship's cook in the Bhendy Bazaar might end its days over a blubber-lamp somewhere on the cool side of the Arctic Circle.

Kadlu, being a good hunter, was rich in iron harpoons, snow-knives, bird-darts, and all the other things that make life easy up there in the great cold; and he was the head of his tribe, or, as they say, "the man who knows all about it by practice." This did not give him any authority, except now and then he could advise his friends to change their hunting-grounds; but Kotuko used it to domineer a little, in the lazy, fat Inuit fashion, over the other boys, when they came out at night to play ball in the moonlight, or to sing the Child's Song to the Aurora Borealis.

But at fourteen an Inuit feels himself a man, and Kotuko was tired of making snares for wild-fowl and kit-foxes, and most tired of all of helping the women to chew seal-and deer-skins (that supples them as nothing else can) the long day through, while the men were out hunting. He wanted to go into the quaggi, the Singing-House, when the hunters gathered there for their mysteries, and the angekok, the sorcerer, frightened them into the most delightful fits after the lamps were put out, and you could hear the Spirit of the Reindeer stamping on the roof; and when a spear was thrust out into the open black night it came back covered with hot blood. He wanted to throw his big boots into the net with the tired air of the head of a family, and to gamble with the hunters when they dropped in of an evening and played a sort of home-made roulette with a tin pot and a nail. There were hundreds of things that he wanted to do, but the grown men laughed at him and said, "Wait till you have been in the buckle, Kotuko. Hunting is not *all* catching."

Now that his father had named a puppy for him, things looked brighter. An Inuit does not waste a good dog on his son till the boy knows something of dog-driving; and Kotuko was more than sure that he knew more than everything.

If the puppy had not had an iron constitution he would have died from overstuffing and overhandling. Kotuko made him a tiny harness with a trace to it, and hauled him all over the house-floor, shouting: "Aua! Ja aua!" (Go to the right). "Choiachoi! Ja choiachoi!" (Go to the left). "Ohaha!" (Stop). The puppy did not like it at all, but being fished for in this way was pure happiness beside being put to the sleigh for the first time. He just sat down on the snow, and played with the seal-hide trace that ran from his harness to the pitu, the big thong in the bows of the sleigh. Then the team started, and the puppy found the heavy ten-foot sleigh running up his back, and dragging him along the snow, while Kotuko laughed till the tears ran down his

face. There followed days and days of the cruel whip
that hisses like the wind over ice, and his companions
all bit him because he did not know his work, and the
harness chafed him, and he was dot allowed to sleep
with Kotuko anymore, but had to take the coldest place
in the passage. It was a sad time for the puppy.

The boy learned, too, as fast as the dog; though a
dog-sleigh is a heart-breaking thing to manage. Each
beast is harnessed, the weakest nearest to the driver, by
his own separate trace, which runs under his left fore-
leg to the main thong, where it is fastened by a sort of
button and loop which can be slipped by a turn of the
wrist, thus freeing one dog at a time. This is very
necessary, because young dogs often get the trace between their hind legs, where it cuts to the bone. And
they one and all *will* go visiting their friends as they
run, jumping in and out among the traces. Then they
fight, and the result is more mixed than a wet fishing-
line next morning. A great deal of trouble can be
avoided by scientific use of the whip. Every Inuit boy
prides himself as being a master of the long lash; but
it is easy to flick at a mark on the ground, and difficult
to lean forward and catch a shirking dog just behind
the shoulders when the sleigh is going at full speed. If
you call one dog's name for "visiting," and accidentally
lash another, the two will fight it out at once, and stop
all the others. Again, if you travel with a companion
and begin to talk, or by yourself and sing, the dogs will
halt, turn round, and sit down to hear what you have
to say. Kotuko was run away from once or twice
through forgetting to block the sleigh when he
stopped; and he broke many lashings, and ruined a few
thongs before he could be trusted with a full team of
eight and the light sleigh. Then he felt himself a person
of consequence, and on smooth, black ice, with a bold
heart and a quick elbow, he smoked along over the

levels as fast as a pack in full cry. He would go ten miles to the seal-holes, and when he was on the hunting-grounds he would twitch a trace loose from the pitu, and free the big black leader, who was the cleverest dog in the team. As soon as the dog had scented a breathing-hole, Kotuko would reverse the sleigh, driving a couple of sawed-off antlers, that stuck up like perambulator-handles from the back-rest, deep into the snow, so that the team could not get away. Then he would crawl forward inch by inch, and wait till the seal came up to breathe. Then he would stab down swiftly with his spear and running-line, and presently would haul his seal up to the lip of the ice, while the black leader came up and helped to pull the carcass across the ice to the sleigh. That was the time when the harnessed dogs yelled and foamed with excitement, and Kotuko laid the long lash like a red-hot bar across all their faces, till the carcass froze stiff. Going home was the heavy work. The loaded sleigh had to be humored among the rough ice, and the dogs sat down and looked hungrily at the seal instead of pulling. At last they would strike the well-worn sleigh-road to the village, and toodle-kiyi along the ringing ice, heads down and tails up, while Kotuko struck up the "Angutivaun tai-na tau-na-ne taina" (The Song of the Returning Hunter), and voices hailed him from house to house under all that dim, star-littern sky.

When Kotuko the dog came to his full growth he enjoyed himself too. He fought his way up the team steadily, fight after fight, till one fine evening, over their food, he tackled the big, black leader (Kotuko the boy saw fair play), and made second dog of him, as they say. So he was promoted to the long thong of the leading dog, running five feet in advance of all the others: it was his bounden duty to stop all fighting, in harness or out of it, and he wore a collar of copper wire, very thick and heavy. On special occasions he was fed with cooked food inside the house, and sometimes was allowed to sleep on the bench with Kotuko. He was a good seal-dog, and would keep a musk-ox at bay by running round him and snapping at his heels. He would even — and this for a sleigh-dog is the last proof of bravery — he would even stand up to the gaunt Arctic wolf, whom all dogs of the North, as a rule, fear beyond anything that walks the snow. He and his master — they did not count the team of ordinary dogs as company — hunted together, day after day and night after night, fur-wrapped boy and savage, long-haired, narrow-eyed, white-fanged, yellow brute. All an Inuit has to do is to get food and skins for himself and his family. The womenfolk make the skins into clothing, and occasionally help in trapping small game; but the bulk of the food — and they eat enormously — must be found by the men. If the supply fails there is no one up there to buy or beg or borrow from. The people must die.

An Inuit does not think of these chances till he is forced to. Kadlu, Kotuko, Amoraq, and the boy-baby who kicked about in Amoraq's fur hood and chewed pieces of blubber all day, were as happy together as any family in the world. They came of a very gentle race — an Inuit seldom loses his temper, and almost never strikes a child — who did not know exactly what telling a real lie meant, still less how to steal. They were content to spear their living out of the heart of the bitter, hopeless cold; to smile oily smiles, and tell queer ghost and fairy tales of evenings, and eat till they could eat no more, and sing the endless woman's song: "Amna aya, aya amna, ah! ah!" through the long lamp-lighted days as they mended their clothes and their hunting-gear.

But one terrible winter everything betrayed them.

The Tununirmiut returned from the yearly salmon-fishing, and made their houses on the early ice to the north of Bylot's Island, ready to go after the seal as soon as the sea froze. But it was an early and savage autumn. All through September there were continuous gales that broke up the smooth seal-ice when it was only four or five feet thick, and forced it inland, and piled a great barrier, some twenty miles broad, of lumped and ragged and needly ice, over which it was impossible to draw the dog-sleighs. The edge of the floe off which the seal were used to fish in winter lay perhaps twenty miles beyond this barrier, and out of reach of the Tununirmiut. Even so, they might have managed to scrape through the winter on their stock of frozen salmon and stored blubber, and what the traps gave them, but in December one of their hunters came across a tupik (a skin-tent) of three women and a girl nearly dead, whose men had come down from the far North and been crushed in their little skin hunting-boats while they were out after the long-horned narwhal. Kadlu, of course, could only distribute the women among the huts of the winter village, for no Inuit dare refuse a meal to a stranger. He never knows when his own turn may come to beg. Amoraq took the girl, who was about fourteen, into her own house as a sort of servant. From the cut of her sharp-pointed hood, and the long diamond pattern of her white deer-skin leggings, they supposed she came from Ellesmere Land. She had never seen tin cooking-pots or wooden-shod sleighs before; but Kotuko the boy and Kotuko the dog were rather fond of her.

Then all the foxes went south, and even the wolverine, that growling, blunt-headed little thief of the snow, did not take the trouble to follow the line of empty traps that Kotuko set. The tribe lost a couple of their best hunters, who were badly crippled in a fight with a musk-ox, and this threw more work on the others. Kotuko went out, day after day, with a light hunting-sleigh and six or seven of the strongest dogs, looking till his eyes ached for some patch of clear ice where a seal might perhaps have scratched a breathing-hole. Kotuko the dog ranged far and wide, and in the dead stillness of the ice-fields Kotuko the boy could hear his half-choked whine of excitement, above a seal-hole three miles away, as plainly as though he were at his elbow. When the dog found a hole the boy would build himself a little, low snow wall to keep off the worst of the bitter wind, and there he would wait ten, twelve, twenty hours for the seal to come up to breathe, his eyes glued to the tiny mark he had made above the hole to guide the downward thrust of his harpoon, a little seal-skin mat under his feet, and his legs tied together in the tutareang (the buckle that the old hunters had talked about). This helps to keep a man's legs from twitching as he waits and waits and waits for the quick-eared seal to rise. Though there is no excitement in it, you can easily believe that the sitting still in the buckle with the thermometer perhaps forty degrees below zero is the hardest work an Inuit knows. When a seal was caught, Kotuko the dog would bound forward, his trace trailing behind him, and help to pull the body to the sleigh, where the tired and hungry dogs lay sullenly under the lee of the broken ice.

A seal did not go very far, for each mouth in the little village had a right to be filled, and neither bone, hide, nor sinew was wasted. The dogs' meat was taken for human use, and Amoraq fed the team with pieces of old summer skin-tents raked out from under the sleeping-bench, and they howled and howled again, and waked to howl hungrily. One could tell by the soap-stone lamps in the huts that famine was near. In good seasons, when blubber was plentiful, the light in the boat-shaped lamps would be two feet high — cheerful, oily, and yellow. Now it was a bare six inches: Amoraq carefully pricked down the moss wick, when an unwatched flame brightened for a moment, and the eyes of all the family followed her hand. The horror of famine up there in the great cold is not so much dying, as dying in the dark. All the Inuit dread the dark that presses on them without a break for six months in each year; and when the lamps are low in the houses the minds of people begin to be shaken and confused.

But worse was to come.

The underfed dogs snapped and growled in the passages, glaring at the cold stars, and snuffing into the bitter wind, night after night. When they stopped howling the silence fell down again as solid and heavy as a snowdrift against a door, and men could hear the beating of their blood in the thin passages of the ear, and the thumping of their own hearts, that sounded as loud as the noise of sorcerers' drums beaten across the snow. One night Kotuko the dog, who had been unusually sullen in harness, leaped up and pushed his head against Kotuko's knee. Kotuko patted him, but the dog still pushed blindly forward, fawning. Then Kadlu waked, and gripped the heavy wolflike head, and stared into the glassy eyes. The dog whimpered and shivered between Kadlu's knees. The hair rose about his neck, and he growled as though a stranger were at the door; then he barked joyously, and rolled on the ground, and bit at Kotuko's boot like a puppy.

"What is it?" said Kotuko; for he was beginning to be afraid.

"The sickness," Kadlu answered. "It is the dog sickness." Kotuko the dog lifted his nose and howled and howled again.

"I have not seen this before. What will he do?" said Kotuko.

Kadlu shrugged one shoulder a little, and crossed the hut for his short stabbing-harpoon. The big dog looked at him, howled again, and slunk away down the passage, while the other dogs drew aside right and left to give him ample room. When he was out on the snow he barked furiously, as though on the trail of a musk-ox, and, barking and leaping and frisking, passed out of sight. His trouble was not hydrophobia, but simple, plain madness. The cold and the hunger, and, above all, the dark, had turned his head; and when the terrible dog-sickness once shows itself in a team, it spreads like wild-fire. Next hunting-day another dog sickened, and was killed then and there by Kotuko as he bit and struggled among the traces. Then the black second dog, who had been the leader in the old days, suddenly gave tongue on an imaginary reindeer-track, and when they slipped him from the pitu he flew at the throat of an ice-cliff, and ran away as his leader had done, his harness on his back. After that no one would take the dogs out again. They needed them for something else, and the dogs knew it; and though they were tied down and fed by hand, their eyes were full of despair and fear. To make things worse, the old women began to tell ghost-tales, and to say that they had met the spirits of the dead hunters lost that autumn, who prophesied all sorts of horrible things.

Kotuko grieved more for the loss of his dog than anything else; for though an Inuit eats enormously he also knows how to starve. But the hunger, the darkness, the cold, and the exposure told on his strength, and he began to hear voices inside his head, and to see people who were not there, out of the tail of his eye. One night – he had unbuckled himself after ten hours' waiting above a "blind" seal-hole, and was staggering back to the village faint and dizzy – he halted to lean his back against a boulder which happened to be supported like a rocking-stone on a single jutting point of ice. His weight disturbed the balance of the thing, it rolled over ponderously, and as Kotuko sprang aside to avoid it, slid after him, squeaking and hissing on the ice-slope.

That was enough for Kotuko. He had been brought up to believe that every rock and boulder had its owner (its inua), who was generally a one-eyed kind of a Woman-Thing called a tornaq, and that when a tornaq meant to help a man she rolled after him inside her stone house, and asked him whether he would take her for a guardian spirit. (In summer thaws the ice-propped rocks and boulders roll and slip all over the face of the land, so you can easily see how the idea of live stones arose.) Kotuko heard the blood beating in his ears as he had heard it all day, and he thought that was the tornaq of the stone speaking to him. Before he reached home he was quite certain that he had held a long conversation with her, and as all his people believed that this was quite possible, no one contradicted him.

"She said to me, 'I jump down, I jump down from my place on the snow,'" cried Kotuko, with hollow eyes, leaning forward in the half-lighted hut. "She said, 'I will be a guide.' She said, 'I will guide you to the good seal-holes.' Tomorrow I go out, and the tornaq will guide me."

Then the angekok, the village sorcerer, came in, and Kotuko told him the tale a second time. It lost nothing in the telling.

"Follow the tornait [the spirits of the stones], and they will bring us food again," said the angekok.

Now the girl from the North had been lying near the lamp, eating very little and saying less for days past; but when Amoraq and Kadlu next morning packed and lashed a little hand-sleigh for Kotuko, and loaded it with his hunting-gear and as much blubber and frozen seal-meat as they could spare, she took the pulling-rope, and stepped out boldly at the boy's side.

"Your house is my house," she said, as the little bone-shod sleigh squeaked and bumped behind them in the awful Arctic night.

"My house is your house," said Kotuko; "but I think that we shall both go to Sedna together."

Now Sedna is the Mistress of the Underworld, and the Inuit believe that everyone who dies must spend a year in her horrible country before going to Quadli-parmiut, the Happy Place, where it never freezes and the fat reindeer trot up when you call.

Through the village people were shouting: "The tor-nait have spoken to Kotuko. They will show him open ice. He will bring us the seal again!" Their voices were soon swallowed up by the cold, empty dark, and Ko-tuko and the girl shouldered close together as they strained on the pulling-rope or humored the sleigh through the ice in the direction of the Polar Sea. Kotuko insisted that the tornaq of the stone had told him to go north, and north they went under Tuktuqd-jung the Reindeer — those stars that we call the Great Bear.

No European could have made five miles a day over the ice-rubbish and the sharp-edged drifts; but those two knew exactly the turn of the wrist that coaxes a sleigh round a hummock, the jerk that nearly lifts it out of an ice-crack, and the exact strength that goes to the few quiet strokes of the spear-head that make a path possible when everything looks hopeless.

The girl said nothing, but bowed her head, and the long wolverine-fur fringe of her ermine hood blew across her broad, dark face. The sky above them was an intense velvety black, changing to bands of Indian red on the horizon, where the great stars burned like street-lamps. From time to time a greenish wave of the Northern Lights would roll across the hollow of the high heavens, flick like a flag, and disappear; or a meteor would crackle from darkness to darkness, trailing a shower of sparks behind. Then they could see the ridged and furrowed surface of the floe tipped and laced with strange colors — red, copper, and bluish; but in the ordinary starlight everything turned to one frost-bitten gray. The floe, as you will remember, had been battered and tormented by the autumn gales till it was one frozen earthquake. There were gullies and ravines, and holes like gravel-pits, cut in ice; lumps and scattered pieces frozen down to the original floor of the floe; blotches of old black ice that had been thrust under the floe in some gale and heaved up again; roundish boulders of ice; sawlike edges of ice carved by the snow that flies before the wind; and sunken pits where thirty or forty acres lay below the level of the rest of the field. From a little distance you might have taken the lumps for seal or walrus, overturned sleighs or men on a hunting expedition, or even the great Ten-legged White Spirit-Bear himself; but in spite of these fantastic shapes, all on the very edge of starting into life, there was neither sound nor the least faint echo of sound. And through this silence and through this waste, where the sudden lights flapped and went out again, the sleigh and the two that pulled it crawled like things in a nightmare — a nightmare of the end of the world at the end of the world.

When they were tired Kotuko would make what the hunters call a "half-house," a very small snow hut, into which they would huddle with the traveling-lamp, and try to thaw out the frozen seal-meat. When they had slept, the march began again — thirty miles a day to get ten miles northward. The girl was always very silent, but Kotuko muttered to himself and broke out into songs he had learned in the Singing-House — summer songs, and reindeer and salmon songs — all horribly out of place at that season. He would declare that he heard the tornaq growling to him, and would run wildly up a hummock, tossing his arms and speaking in loud, threatening tones. To tell the truth, Kotuko was very nearly crazy for the time being; but the girl was sure that he was being guided by his guardian spirit, and that everything would come right. She was not surprised, therefore, when at the end of the fourth march Kotuko, whose eyes were burning like fire-balls in his head, told her that his tornaq was following them across the snow in the shape of a two-headed dog. The girl looked where Kotuko pointed, and something seemed to slip into a ravine. It was certainly not human, but everybody knew that the tornait preferred to appear in the shape of bear and seal, and such like.

It might have been the Ten-legged White Spirit-Bear himself, or it might have been anything, for Kotuko and the girl were so starved that their eyes were untrustworthy. They had trapped nothing, and seen no trace of game since they had left the village; their food would not hold out for another week, and there was a gale coming. A Polar storm can blow for ten days without a break, and all that while it is certain death to be abroad. Kotuko laid up a snow-house large enough to take in the hand-sleigh (never be separated from your meat), and while he was shaping the last irregular block of ice that makes the keystone of the roof, he saw a Thing looking at him from a little cliff of ice half a mile away. The air was hazy, and the Thing seemed to be forty feet long and ten feet high, with twenty feet of tail and a shape that quivered all along the outlines. The girl saw it too, but instead of crying aloud with terror, said quietly, "That is Quiquern. What comes after?"

"He will speak to me," said Kotuko; but the snow-knife trembled in his hand as he spoke, because however much a man may believe that he is a friend of strange and ugly spirits, he seldom likes to be taken quite at his word. Quiquern, too, is the phantom of a gigantic toothless dog without any hair, who is supposed to live in the far North, and to wander about the country just before things are going to happen. They may be pleasant or unpleasant things, but not even the sorcerers care to speak about Quiquern. He makes the dogs go mad. Like the Spirit-Bear, he has several extra pairs of legs, — six or eight, — and this Thing jumping up and down in the haze had more legs than any real dog needed. Kotuko and the girl huddled into their hut quickly. Of course if Quiquern had wanted them, he could have torn it to pieces above their heads, but the sense of a foot-thick snow-wall between themselves and the wicked dark was great comfort. The gale broke with a shriek of wind like the shriek of a train, and for three days and three nights it held, never varying one point, and never lulling even for a minute. They fed the stone lamp between their knees, and nibbled at the half-warm seal-meat, and watched the black soot gather on the roof for seventy-two long hours. The girl counted up the food in the sleigh; there was not more than two days' supply, and Kotuko looked over the iron heads and the deer-sinew fastenings of his harpoon and his seal-lance and his bird-dart. There was nothing else to do.

"We shall go to Sedna soon — very soon," the girl whispered. "In three days we shall lie down and go. Will your tornaq do nothing? Sing her an angekok's song to make her come here."

He began to sing in the high-pitched howl of the magic songs, and the gale went down slowly. In the middle of his song the girl started, laid her mittened hand and then her head to the ice floor of the hut. Kotuko followed her example, and the two kneeled, staring into each other's eyes, and listening with every nerve. He ripped a thin sliver of whalebone from the rim of a bird-snare that lay on the sleigh, and, after straightening, set it upright in a little hole in the ice, firming it down with his mitten. It was almost as delicately adjusted as a compass-needle, and now instead of listening they watched. The thin rod quivered a little — the least little jar in the world; then it vibrated steadily for a few seconds, came to rest, and vibrated again, this time nodding to another point of the compass.

"Too soon!" said Kotuko. "Some big floe has broken far away outside."

The girl pointed at the rod, and shook her head. "It is the big breaking," she said. "Listen to the ground-ice. It knocks."

When they kneeled this time they heard the most curious muffled grunts and knockings, apparently under their feet. Sometimes it sounded as though a blind puppy were squeaking above the lamp; then as if a stone were being ground on hard ice; and again, like muffled blows on a drum; but all dragged out and made small, as though they traveled through a little horn a weary distance away.

"We shall not go to Sedna lying down," said Kotuko. "It is the breaking. The tornaq has cheated us. We shall die."

All this may sound absurd enough, but the two were face to face with a very real danger. The three days' gale had driven the deep water of Baffin's Bay southerly, and piled it on to the edge of the far-reaching land-ice that stretches from Bylot's Island to the west. Also, the strong current which sets east out of Lancaster Sound carried with it mile upon mile of what they call pack-ice — rough ice that has not frozen into fields; and this pack was bombarding the floe at the same time that the swell and heave of the storm-worked sea was weakening and undermining it. What Kotuko and the girl had been listening to were the faint echoes of that fight thirty or forty miles away, and the little tell-tale rod quivered to the shock of it.

Now, as the Inuit say, when the ice once wakes after its long winter sleep, there is no knowing what may happen, for solid floe-ice changes shape almost as quickly as a cloud. The gale was evidently a spring gale sent out of time, and anything was possible.

Yet the two were happier in their minds than before. If the floe broke up there would be no more waiting and suffering. Spirits, goblins, and witch-people were moving about on the racking ice, and they might find themselves stepping into Sedna's countryside by side with all sorts of wild Things, the flush of excitement still on them. When they left the hut after the gale, the noise on the horizon was steadily growing, and the tough ice moaned and buzzed all round them.

"It is still waiting," said Kotuko.

On the top of a hummock sat or crouched the eight-legged Thing that they had seen three days before – and it howled horribly.

"Let us follow," said the girl. "It may know some way that does not lead to Sedna"; but she reeled from weakness as she took the pulling-rope. The Thing moved off slowly and clumsily across the ridges, heading always toward the westward and the land, and they followed, while the growling thunder at the edge of the floe rolled nearer and nearer. The floe's lip was split and cracked in every direction for three or four miles inland, and great pans of ten-foot-thick ice, from a few yards to twenty acres square, were jolting and ducking and surging into one another, and into the yet unbroken floe, as the heavy swell took and shook and spouted between them. This battering-ram ice was, so to speak, the first army that the sea was flinging against the floe. The incessant crash and jar of these cakes almost drowned the ripping sound of sheets of pack-ice driven bodily under the floe as cards are hastily pushed under a tablecloth. Where the water was shallow these sheets would be piled one atop of the other till the bottommost touched mud fifty feet down, and the discolored sea banked behind the muddy ice till the increasing pressure drove all forward again. In addition to the floe and the pack-ice, the gale and the currents were bringing down true bergs, sailing mountains of ice, snapped off from the Greenland side of the water or the north shore of Melville Bay. They pounded in solemnly, the waves breaking white round them, and advanced on the floe like an old-time fleet under full sail. A berg that seemed ready to carry the world before it would ground helplessly in deep water, reel over, and wallow in a lather of foam and mud and flying frozen spray, while a much smaller and lower one would rip and ride into the flat floe, flinging tons of ice on either side, and cutting a track half a mile long before it was stopped. Some fell like swords, shearing a raw-edged canal; and others splintered into a shower of blocks, weighing scores of tons apiece, that whirled and skirted among the hummocks. Others, again, rose up bodily out of the water when they shoaled, twisted as though in pain, and fell solidly on their sides, while the sea threshed over their shoulders. This trampling and crowding and bending and buckling and arching of the ice into every possible shape was going on as far as the eye could reach all along the north line of the floe. From where Kotuko and the girl were, the confusion looked no more than an uneasy, rippling, crawling movement under the horizon; but it came toward them each moment, and they could hear, far away to land-ward a heavy booming, as it might have been the boom of artillery through a fog. That showed that the floe was being jammed home against the iron cliffs of Bylot's Island, the land to the southward behind them.

"This has never been before," said Kotuko, staring stupidly. "This is not the time. How can the floe break *now?*"

"Follow *that!* the girl cried, pointing to the Thing half limping, half running distractedly before them. They followed, tugging at the hand-sleigh, while nearer and nearer came the roaring march of the ice. At last the fields round them cracked and starred in every direction, and the cracks opened and snapped like the teeth of wolves. But where the Thing rested, on a mound of old and scattered ice-blocks some fifty feet high, there was no motion. Kotuko leaped forward wildly, dragging the girl after him, and crawled to the bottom of the mound. The talking of the ice grew louder and louder round them, but the mound stayed fast, and, as the girl looked at him, he threw his right elbow upward and outward, making the Inuit sign for land in the shape of an island. And land it was that the eight-legged, limping Thing had led them to — some granite-tipped, sand-beached islet off the coast, shod and sheathed and masked with ice so that no man could have told it from the floe, but at the bottom solid earth, and not shifting ice! The smashing and rebound of the floes as they grounded and splintered marked the borders of it, and a friendly shoal ran out to the northward, and turned aside the rush of the heaviest ice, exactly as a ploughshare turns over loam. There was danger, of course, that some heavily squeezed ice-field might shoot up the beach, and plane off the top of the islet bodily; but that did not trouble Kotuko and the girl when they made their snow-house and began to eat, and heard the ice hammer and skid along the beach. The Thing had disappeared, and Kotuko was talking excitedly about his power over spirits as he crouched round the lamp. In the middle of his wild sayings the girl began to laugh, and rock herself backward and forward.

Behind her shoulder, crawling into the hut crawl by crawl, there were two heads, one yellow and one black, that belonged to two of the most sorrowful and ashamed dogs that ever you saw. Kotuko the dog was one, and the black leader was the other. Both were now fat, well-looking, and quite restored to their proper minds, but coupled to each other in an extraordinary fashion. When the black leader ran off, you remember, his harness was still on him. He must have met Kotuko the dog, and played or fought with him, for his shoulder-loop had caught in the plaited copper wire of Kotuko's collar, and had drawn tight, so that neither could get at the trace to gnaw it apart, but each was fastened sidelong to his neighbor's neck. That, with the freedom of hunting on their own account, must have helped to cure their madness. They were very sober.

The girl pushed the two shamefaced creatures towards Kotuko, and, sobbing with laughter, cried, "That is Quiquern, who led us to safe ground. Look at his eight legs and double head!"

Kotuko cut them free, and they fell into his arms, yellow and black together, trying to explain how they had got their senses back again. Kotuko ran a hand down their ribs, which were round and well clothed. "They have found food," he said, with a grin. "I do not think we shall go to Sedna so soon. My tornaq sent these. The sickness has left them."

As soon as they had greeted Kotuko, these two, who had been forced to sleep and eat and hunt together for the past few weeks, flew at each other's throat, and there was a beautiful battle in the snow-house. "Empty dogs do not fight," Kotuko said. "They have found the seal. Let us sleep. We shall find food."

When they waked there was open water on the north beach of the island, and all the loosened ice had been driven landward. The first sound of the surf is one of the most delightful that the Inuit can hear, for it means that spring is on the road. Kotuko and the girl took hold of hands and smiled, for the clear, full roar of the surge among the ice reminded them of salmon and reindeer time and the smell of blossoming ground-willows. Even as they looked, the sea began to skim over between the floating cakes of ice, so intense was the cold; but on the horizon there was a vast red glare, and that was the light of the sunken sun. It was more like hearing him yawn in his sleep than seeing him rise, and the glare lasted for only a few minutes, but it marked the turn of the year. Nothing, they felt, could alter that.

Kotuko found the dogs fighting over a fresh-killed seal who was following the fish that a gale always disturbs. He was the first of some twenty or thirty seal that landed on the island in the course of the day, and till the sea froze hard there were hundreds of keen black heads rejoicing in the shallow free water and floating about with the floating ice.

It was good to eat seal-liver again; to fill the lamps recklessly with blubber, and watch the flame blaze three feet in the air; but as soon as the new sea-ice bore, Kotuko and the girl loaded the hand-sleigh, and made the two dogs pull as they had never pulled in their lives, for they feared what might have happened in their village. The weather was as pitiless as usual; but it is easier to draw a sleigh loaded with good food than to hunt starving. They left five-and-twenty seal carcasses buried in the ice of the beach, all ready for use, and hurried back to their people. The dogs showed them the way as soon as Kotuko told them what was expected, and though there was no sign of a landmark, in two days they were giving tongue outside Kadlu's house. Only three dogs answered them; the others had been eaten, and the houses were all dark. But when Kotuko shouted, "Ojo!" (boiled meat), weak voices replied, and when he called the muster of the village name by name, very distinctly, there were no gaps in it.

An hour later the lamps blazed in Kadlu's house; snow-water was heating; the pots were beginning to simmer, and the snow was dripping from the roof, as Amoraq made ready a meal for all the village, and the boy-baby in the hood chewed at a strip of rich nutty blubber, and the hunters slowly and methodically filled themselves to the very brim with seal-meat. Kotuko and the girl told their tale. The two dogs sat between them, and whenever their names came in, they cocked an ear apiece and looked most thoroughly ashamed of themselves. A dog who has once gone mad and recovered, the Inuit say, is safe against all further attacks.

"So the tornaq did not forget us," said Kotuko. "The storm blew, the ice broke, and the seal swam in behind the fish that were frightened by the storm. Now the new seal-holes are not two days distant. Let the good hunters go tomorrow and bring back the seal I have speared — twenty-five seal buried in the ice. When we have eaten those we will all follow the seal on the floe."

"What do *you* do?" said the sorcerer in the same sort of voice as he used to Kadlu, richest of the Tununir-miut.

Kadlu looked at the girl from the North, and said quietly, "*We* build a house." He pointed to the north-west side of Kadlu's house, for that is the side on which the married son or daughter always lives.

The girl turned her hands palm upward, with a little despairing shake of her head. She was a foreigner, picked up starving, and could bring nothing to the housekeeping.

Amoraq jumped from the bench where she sat, and began to sweep things into the girl's lap — stone lamps, iron skin-scrapers, tin kettles, deer-skins embroidered with musk-ox teeth, and real canvas-needles such as sailors use — the finest dowry that has ever been given on the far edge of the Arctic Circle, and the girl from the North bowed her head down to the very floor.

"Also these!" said Kotuko, laughing and signing to the dogs, who thrust their cold muzzles into the girl's face.

"Ah," said the angekok, with an important cough, as though he had been thinking it all over. "As soon as Kotuko left the village I went to the Singing-House and sang magic. I sang all the long nights, and called upon the Spirit of the Reindeer. *My* singing made the gale blow that broke the ice and drew the two dogs toward Kotuko when the ice would have crushed his bones. *My* song drew the seal in behind the broken ice. My body lay still in the quaggi, but my spirit ran about on the ice, and guided Kotuko and the dogs in all the things they did. I did it."

Everybody was full and sleepy, so no one contradicted; and the angekok, by virtue of his office, helped himself to yet another lump of boiled meat, and lay down to sleep with the others in the warm, well-lighted, oil-smelling home.

*N*ow Kotuko, who drew very well in the Inuit fashion, scratched pictures of all these adventures on a long, flat piece of ivory with a hole at one end. When he and the girl went north to Ellesmere Land in the year of the Wonderful Open Winter, he left the picture-story with Kadlu, who lost it in the shingle when his dog-sleigh broke down one summer on the beach of Lake Netilling at Nikosiring, and there a Lake Inuit found it next spring and sold it to a man at Imigen who was interpreter on a Cumberland Sound whaler, and he sold it to Hans Olsen, who was afterward a quartermaster on board a big steamer that took tourists to the North Cape in Norway. When the tourist season was over, the steamer ran between London and Australia, stopping at Ceylon, and there Olsen sold the ivory to a Cingalese jeweler for two imitation sapphires. I found it under some rubbish in a house at Colombo, and have translated it from one end to the other.

'Angutivaun Taina'

[This is a very free translation of the Song of the Returning Hunter, as the men used to sing it after seal-spearing. The Inuit always repeat things over and over again.]

Our gloves are stiff with the frozen blood,
   Our furs with the drifted snow,
As we come in with the seal — the seal!
   In from the edge of the floe.

Au jana! Aua! Oha! Haq!
   And the yelping dog-teams go,
And the long whips crack, and the men come back,
   Back from the edge of the floe !

We tracked our seal to his secret place,
   We heard him scratch below,
We made our mark, and we watched beside,
   Out on the edge of the floe.

We raised our lance when he rose to breathe,
   We drove it downward — so!
And we played him thus, and we killed him thus,
   Out on the edge of the floe.

Our gloves are glued with the frozen blood,
    Our eyes with the drifting snow;
But we come back to our wives again,
    Back from the edge of the floe!

Au jana! Aua! Oha! Haq!
    And the loaded dog-teams go,
And the wives can hear their men come back.
    Back from the edge of the floe!

Red Dog

For our white and our excellent nights — -for the
     nights of swift running.
    Fair ranging, far seeing, good hunting, sure
     cunning!
For the smells of the dawning, untainted, ere dew
     has departed!
For the rush through the mist, and the quarry
     blind-started!
For the cry of our mates when the sambhur has
     wheeled and is standing at bay,
        For the risk and the riot of night!
        For the sleep at the lair-mouth by day,
        It is met, and we go to the fight.
                Bay! O Bay!

*I*t was after the letting in of the Jungle that the pleasantest part of Mowgli's life began. He had the good conscience that comes from paying debts; all the Jungle was his friend, and just a little afraid of him. The things that he did and saw and heard when he was wandering from one people to another, with or without his four companions, would make many many stories, each as long as this one. So you will never be told how he met the Mad Elephant of Mandla, who killed two-and-twenty bullocks drawing eleven carts of coined silver to the Government Treasury, and scattered the shiny rupees in the dust; how he fought Jacala, the Crocodile, all one long night in the Marshes of the North, and broke his skinning-knife on the brute's back-plates; how he found a new and longer knife round the neck of a man who had been killed by a wild boar, and how he tracked that boar and killed him as a fair price for the knife; how he was caught up once in the Great Famine, by the moving of the deer, and nearly crushed to death in the swaying hot herds; how he saved Hathi the Silent from being once more trapped in a pit with a stake at the bottom, and how, next day, he himself fell into a very cunning leopard-trap, and how Hathi broke the thick wooden bars to pieces above him; how he milked the wild buffaloes in the swamp, and how —

But we must tell one tale at a time. Father and Mother Wolf died, and Mowgli rolled a big boulder against the mouth of their cave, and cried the Death Song over them; Baloo grew very old and stiff, and even Bagheera, whose nerves were steel and whose muscles were iron, was a shade slower on the kill than he had been. Akela turned from gray to milky white with pure age; his ribs stuck out, and he walked as though he had been made of wood, and Mowgli killed for him. But the young wolves, the children of the disbanded Seeonee Pack, throve and increased, and when there were about forty of them, masterless, full-voiced, clean-footed five-year-olds, Akela told them that they ought to gather themselves together ahd follow the Law, and run under one head, as befitted the Free People.

This was not a question in which Mowgli concerned

himself, for, as he said, he had eaten sour fruit, and he knew the tree it hung from; but when Phao, son of Phaona (his father was the Gray Tracker in the days of Akela's headship), fought his way to the leadership of the Pack, according to the Jungle Law, and the old calls and songs began to ring under the stars once more, Mowgli came to the Council Rock for memory's sake. When he chose to speak the Pack waited till he had finished, and he sat at Akela's side on the rock above Phao. Those were days of good hunting and good sleeping. No stranger cared to break into the jungles that belonged to Mowgli's people, as they called the Pack, and the young wolves grew fat and strong, and there were many cubs to bring to the Looking-over. Mowgli always attended a Looking-over, remembering the night when a black panther bought a naked brown baby into the pack, and the long call, "Look, look well, O Wolves," made his heart flutter. Otherwise, he would be far away in the Jungle with his four brothers, tasting, touching, seeing, and feeling new things.

One twilight when he was trotting leisurely across the ranges to give Akela the half of a buck that he had killed, while the Four jogged behind him, sparring a little, and tumbling one another over for joy of being alive, he heard a cry that had never been heard since the bad days of Shere Khan. It was what they call in the Jungle the pheeal, a hideous kind of shriek that the jackal gives when he is hunting behind a tiger, or when there is a big killing afoot. If you can imagine a mixture of hate, triumph, fear, and despair, with a kind of leer running through it, you will get some notion of the pheeal that rose and sank and wavered and quavered far away across the Waingunga. The Four stopped at once, bristling and growling. Mowgli's hand went to his knife, and he checked, the blood in his face, his eyebrows knotted.

"There is no Striped One dare kill here," he said.

"That is not the cry of the Forerunner," answered Gray Brother. "It is some great killing. Listen!"

It broke out again, half sobbing and half chuckling, just as though the jackal had soft human lips. Then Mowgli drew deep breath, and ran to the Council Rock, overtaking on his way hurrying wolves of the Pack. Phao and Akela were on the Rock together, and below them, every nerve strained, sat the others. The mothers and the cubs were cantering off to their lairs; for when the pheeal cries it is no time for weak things to be abroad.

They could hear nothing except the Waingunga rushing and gurgling in the dark, and the light evening winds among the tree-tops, till suddenly across the river a wolf called. It was no wolf of the Pack, for they were all at the Rock. The note changed to a long, despairing bay; and "Dhole!" it said, "Dhole! dhole! dhole!" They heard tired feet on the rocks, and a gaunt wolf, streaked with red on his flanks, his right fore-paw useless, and his jaws white with foam, flung himself into the circle and lay gasping at Mowgli's feet.

"Good hunting! Under whose Headship?" said Phao gravely.

"Good hunting! Won-tolla am I," was the answer. He meant that he was a solitary wolf, fending for himself, his mate, and his cubs in some lonely lair, as do many wolves in the south. Won-tolla means an Outlier — one who lies out from any Pack. Then he panted, and they could see his heart-beats shake him backward and forward.

"What moves?" said Phao, for that is the question all the Jungle asks after the pheeal cries.

"The dhole, the dhole of the Dekkan — Red Dog, the Killer! They came north from the south saying the Dekkan was empty and killing out by the way. When this moon was new there were four to me — my mate and three cubs. She would teach them to kill on the grass plains, hiding to drive the buck, as we do who are of the open. At midnight I heard them together, full tongue on the trail. At the dawn-wind I found them stiff in the grass — four, Free People, four when this moon was new. Then sought I my Blood-Right and found the dhole."

"How many?" said Mowgli quickly; the Pack growled deep in their throats.

"I do not know. Three of them will kill no more, but at the last they drove me like the buck; on my three legs they drove me. Look, Free People!"

He thrust out his mangled fore-foot, all dark with dried blood. There were cruel bites low down on his side, and his throat was torn and worried.

"Eat," said Akela, rising up from the meat Mowgli had brought him, and the Outlier flung himself on it.

"This shall be no loss," he said humbly, when he had taken off the first edge of his hunger. "Give me a little strength, Free People, and I also will kill. My lair is empty that was full when this moon was new, and the Blood Debt is not all paid."

Phao heard his teeth crack on a haunch-bone and grunted approvingly.

"We shall need those jaws," said he. "Were there cubs with the dhole?"

"Nay, nay. Red Hunters all: grown dogs of their Pack, heavy and strong for all that they eat lizards in the Dekkan."

What Won-tolla had said meant that the dhole, the red hunting-dog of the Dekkan, was moving to kill, and the Pack knew well that even the tiger will surrender a new kill to the dhole. They drive straight through the Jungle, and what they meet they pull down and tear to pieces. Though they are not as big nor half as cunning as the wolf, they are very strong and very numerous. The dhole, for instance, do not begin to call themselves a pack till they are a hundred strong; whereas forty wolves make a very fair pack indeed. Mowgli's wanderings had taken him to the edge of the high grassy downs of the Dekkan, and he had seen the fearless dholes sleeping and playing and scratching themselves in the little hollows and tussocks that they use for lairs. He despised and hated them because they did not smell like the Free People, because they did not live in caves, and, above all, because they had hair between their toes while he and his friends were clean-footed. But he knew, for Hathi had told him, what a terrible thing a dhole hunting-pack was. Even Hathi moves aside from their line, and until they are killed, or till game is scarce, they will go forward.

Akela knew something of the dholes, too, for he said to Mowgli quietly, "It is better to die in a Full Pack than leaderless and alone. This is good hunting, and – my last. But, as men live, thou hast very manymore nights and days, Little Brother. Go north and lie down, and if any live after the dhole has gone by he shall bring thee word of the fight."

"*A*h," said Mowgli, quite gravely, "must I go to the marshes and catch little fish and sleep in a tree, or must I ask help of the Bandar-log and crack nuts, while the Pack fight below?"

"It is to the death," said Akela. "Thou hast never met the dhole – the Red Killer. Even the Striped One –"

"Aowa! Aowa!" said Mowgli pettingly. "I have killed one striped ape, and sure am I in my stomach that Shere Khan would have left his own mate for meat to the dhole if he had winded a pack across three ranges.

Listen now: There was a wolf, my father, and there was a wolf, my mother, and there was an old gray wolf (not too wise: he is white now) was my father and my mother. Therefore I —" he raised his voice, "I say that when the dhole come, and if the dhole come, Mowgli and the Free People are of one skin for that hunting ; and I say, by the Bull that bought me — by the Bull Bagheera paid for me in the old days which ye of the Pack do not remember — *I* say, that the Trees and the River may hear and hold fast if I forget; *I* say that this my knife shall be as a tooth to the Pack — and I do not think it is so blunt. This is my Word which has gone from me."

"Thou dost not know the dhole, man with a wolf's tongue," said Won-tolla. "I look only to clear the Blood Debt against them ere they have me in many pieces. They move slowly, killing out as they go, but in two days a little strength will come back to me and I turn again for the Blood Debt. But for *ye*, Free People, my word is that ye go north and eat but little for a while till the dhole are gone. There is no meat in this hunting."

"Hear the Outlier!" said Mowgli with a laugh. "Free People, we must go north and dig lizards and rats from the bank, lest by any chance we meet the dhole. He must kill out our hunting-grounds, while we lie hid in the north till it please him to give us our own again. He is a dog — and the pup of a dog — red, yellow-bellied, lairless, and haired between every toe! He counts his cubs six and eight at the litter, as though he were Chikai, the little leaping rat. Surely we must run away, Free People, and beg leave of the peoples of the north for the offal of dead cattle! Ye know the saying: 'North are the vermin; south are the lice. *We* are the Jungle.' Choose ye, O choose. It is good hunting! For the Pack — for the Full Pack — for the lair and the litter; for the in-kill and the out-kill; for the mate that drives the doe and the little, little cub within the cave; it is met! — it is met! — it is met!"

The Pack answered with one deep, crashing bark that sounded in the night like a big tree falling. "It is met!" they cried. "Stay with these," said Mowgli to the Four. "We shall need every tooth. Phao and Akela must make ready the battle. I go to count the dogs."

"It is death!" Won-tolla cried, half rising. "What can such a hairless one do against the Red Dog? Even the Striped One, remember —"

"Thou art indeed an Outlier," Mowgli called back; "but we will speak when the dholes are dead. Good hunting all!"

He hurried off into the darkness, wild with excitement, hardly looking where he set foot, and the natural consequence was that he tripped full length over Kaa's great coils where the python lay watching a deer-path near the river.

"Kssha!" said Kaa angrily. "Is this jungle-work, to stamp and tramp and undo a night's hunting — when the game are moving so well, too?"

"The fault was mine," said Mowgli, picking himself up. "Indeed I was seeking thee, Flathead, but each time we meet thou art longer and broader by the length of my arm. There is none like thee in the Jungle, wise, old, strong, and most beautiful Kaa."

"Now whither does *this* trail lead?" Kaa's voice was gentler. "Not a moon since there was a Manling with a knife threw stones at my head and called me bad little tree-cat names, because I lay asleep in the open."

"Aye, and turned every driven deer to all the winds, and Mowgli was hunting, and this same Flathead was too deaf to hear his whistle, and leave the deer-roads free," Mowgli answered composedly, sitting down among the painted coils.

"Now this same Manling comes with soft, tickling words to this same Flathead, telling him that he is wise and strong and beautiful, and this same old Flathead believes and makes a place, thus, for this same stone-throwing Manling, and — Art thou at ease now? Could Bagheera give thee so good a resting-place?"

Kaa had, as usual, made a sort of soft half-hammock of himself under Mowgli's weight. The boy reached out in the darkness, and gathered in the supple cable-like neck till Kaa's head rested on his shoulder, and then he told him all that had happened in the Jungle that night.

"Wise I may be," said Kaa at the end; "but deaf I surely am. Else I should have heard the pheeal. Small wonder the Eaters of Grass are uneasy. How many be the dhole?"

"I have not yet seen. I came hot-foot to thee. Thou art older than Hathi. But oh, Kaa," — here Mowgli wriggled with sheerjoy, — "it will be good hunting. Few of us will see another moon."

"Dost *thou* strike in this? Remember thou art a Man; and remember what Pack cast thee out. Let the Wolf look to the Dog. *thou* art a Man."

"Last year's nuts are this year's black earth," said Mowgli. "It is true that I am a Man, but it is in my stomach that this night I have said that I am a Wolf. I called the River and the Trees to remember. I am of the Free People, Kaa, till the dhole has gone by."

"Free People," Kaa grunted. "Free thieves! And thou hast tied thyself into the death-knot for the sake of the memory of the dead wolves? This is no good hunting."

"It is my Word which I have spoken. The Trees know, the River knows. Till the dhole have gone by my Word comes not back to me."

"Ngssh! This changes all trails. I had thought to take thee away with me to the northern marshes, but the

Word — even the Word of a little, naked, hairless
Manling — is the Word. Now I, Kaa, say —"

"Think well, Flathead, lest thou tie thyself into the
death-knot also. I need no Word from thee, for well I
know —"

"Be it so, then," said Kaa. "I will give no Word; but
what is in thy stomach to do when the dhole come?"

"They must swim the Waingunga. I thought to meet
them with my knife in the shallows, the Pack behind
me; and so stabbing and thrusting, we a little might
turn them down-stream, or cool their throats."

"The dhole do not turn and their throats are hot,"
said Kaa. "There will be neither Manling nor Wolf-cub
when that hunting is done, but only dry bones."

"Alala! If we die, we die. It will be most good hunting. But my stomach is young, and I have not seen
many Rains. I am not wise nor strong. Hast thou a
better plan, Kaa?"

"I have seen a hundred and a hundred Rains. Ere
Hathi cast his milk-tushes my trail was big in the dust.
By the First Egg, I am older than many trees, and I
have seen all that the Jungle has done."

"But *this* is new hunting," said Mowgli. "Never before have the dhole crossed our trail."

"What is has been. What will be is no more than a
forgotten year striking backward. Be still while I count
those my years."

For a long hour Mowgli lay back among the coils,
while Kaa, his head motionless on the ground, thought
of all that he had seen and known since the day he
came from the egg. The light seemed to go out of his
eyes and leave them like stale opals, and now and again
he made little stiff passes with his head, right and left,
as though he were hunting in his sleep. Mowgli dozed
quietly, for he knew that there is nothing like sleep
before hunting, and he was trained to take it at any

hour of the day or night.

Then he felt Kaa's back grow bigger and broader below him as the huge python puffed himself out, hissing with the noise of a sword drawn from a steel scabbard.

"I have seen all the dead seasons," Kaa said at last, "and the great trees and the old elephants, and the rocks that were bare and sharp-pointed ere the moss grew. Art *thou* still alive, Manling?"

"It is only a little after moonset," said Mowgli. I do not understand — "

"Hssh! I am again Kaa. I knew it was but a little time. Now we will go to the river, and I will show thee what is to be done against the dhole."

He turned, straight as an arrow, for the main stream of the Waingunga, plunging in a little above the pool that hid the Peace Rock, Mowgli at his side.

"Nay, do not swim. I go swiftly. My back, Little Brother."

Mowgli tucked his left arm round Kaa's neck, dropped his right close to his body, and straightened his feet. Then Kaa breasted the current as he alone could, and the ripple of the checked water stood up in a frill round Mowgli's neck, and his feet were waved to and fro in the eddy under the python's lashing sides. A mile or two above the Peace Rock the Waingunga narrows between a gorge of marble rocks from eighty to a hundred feet high, and the current runs like a mill-race between and over all manner of ugly stones. But Mowgli did not trouble his head about the water; little water in the world could have given him a moment's fear. He was looking at the gorge on either side and sniffing uneasily, for there was a sweetish-sourish smell in the air, very like the smell of a big anthill on a hot day. Instinctively he lowered himself in the water, only raising his head to breathe from time to time, and

Kaa came to anchor with a double twist of his tail round a sunken rock, holding Mowgli in the hollow of a coil, while the water raced on.

"This is the Place of Death," said the boy. "Why do we come here?"

"They sleep," said Kaa. "Hathi will not turn aside for the Striped One. Yet Hathi and the Striped One together turn aside for the dhole, and the dhole they say turn aside for nothing. And yet for whom do the Little People of the Rocks turn aside? Tell me, Master of the Jungle, who is the Master of the Jungle?"

"These," Mowgli whispered. "It is the Place of Death. Let us go."

"Nay, look well, for they are asleep. It is as it was when I was not the length of thy arm."

The split and weatherworn rocks of the gorge of the Waingunga had been used since the beginning of the Jungle by the Little People of the Rocks — the busy, furious, black wild bees of India; and, as Mowgli knew well, all trails turned off half a mile before they reached the gorge. For centuries the Little People had hived and swarmed from cleft to cleft, and swarmed again, staining the white marble with stale honey, and made their combs tall and deep in the dark of the inner caves, where neither man nor beast nor fire nor water had ever touched them. The length of the gorge on both siaes was hung as it were with black shimmery velvet curtains, and Mowgli sank as he looked, for those were the clotted millions of the sleeping bees. There were other lumps and festoons and things like decayed tree-trunks studded on the face of the rock, the old combs of past years, or new cities built in the shadow of the windless gorge, and huge masses of spongy, rotten trash had rolled down and stuck among the trees and creepers that clung to the rock-face. As he listened he heard more than once the rustle and slide of a

honey-loaded comb turning over or failing away somewhere in the dark galleries; then a booming of angry
wings, and the sullen drip, drip, drip, of the wasted
honey, guttering along till it lipped over some ledge in
the open air and sluggishly trickled down on the twigs.
There was a tiny little beach, not five feet broad, on
one side of the river, and that was piled high with the
rubbish of uncounted years. There were dead bees,
drones, sweepings, and stale combs, and wings of ma-
rauding moths that had strayed in after honey, all
tumbled in smooth piles of the finest black dust. The
mere sharp smell of it was enough to frighten anything
that had no wings, and knew what the Little People
were.

Kaa moved up-stream again till he came to a sandy
bar at the head of the gorge.

"Here is this season's kill," said he. "Look!" On the
bank lay the skeletons of a couple of young deer and
a buffalo. Mowgli could see that neither wolf nor jackal
had touched the hones, which were laid out naturally.

"They came beyond the line;, they did not know the
Law," murmured Mowgli, "and the Little People killed
them. Let us go ere they wake."

"They do not wake till the dawn," said Kaa. "Now I
will tell thee. A hunted buck from the south, many,
many Rains ago, came hither from the south, not
knowing the Jungle, a Pack on his trail. Being made
blind by fear, he leaped from above, the Pack running
by sight, for they were hot and blind on the trail. The
sun was high, and the Little People were many and very
angry. Many, too, were those of the Pack who leaped
into the Waingunga, but they were dead ere they took
water. Those who did not leap died also in the rocks
above. But the buck lived."

"How?"

"Because he came first, running for his life, leaping

ere the Little People were aware, and was in the river when they gathered to kill. The Pack, following, was altogether lost under the weight of the Little People."

"The buck lived?" Mowgli repeated slowly.

"At least he did not die *then*, though none waited his coming down with a strong body to hold him safe against the water, as a certain old fat, deaf, yellow Flathead would wait for a Manling — yea, though there were all the dholes of the Dekkan on his trail. What is in thy stomach?" Kaa's head was close to Mowgli's ear; and it was a little time before the boy answered.

"It is to pull the very whiskers of Death, but — Kaa, thou art, indeed, the wisest of all the Jungle."

"So many have said. Look now, if the dhole follow thee —"

"As surely they will follow. Ho! ho! I have many little thorns under my tongue to prick into their hides."

"If they follow thee hot and blind, looking only at thy shoulders, those who do not die up above will take water either here or lower down, for the Little People will rise up and cover them. Now the Waingunga is hungry water, and they will have no Kaa to hold them, but will go down, such as live, to the shallows by the Seeonee Lairs, and there thy Pack may meet them by the throat."

"Ahai! Eowawa! Better could not be till the Rains fall in the dry season. There is now only the little matter of the run and the leap. I will make me known to the dholes, so that they shall follow me very closely."

"Hast thou seen the rocks above thee? From the landward side?"

"Indeed, no. That I had forgotten."

"Go look. It is all rotten ground, cut and full of holes. One of thy clumsy feet set down without seeing would end the hunt. See, I leave thee here, and for thy sake only I will carry word to the Pack that they may know where to look for the dhole. For myself, I am not of one skin with *any* wolf."

When Kaa disliked an acquaintance he could be more unpleasant than any of the Jungle People, except perhaps Bagheera. He swam down-stream, and opposite the Rock he came on Phao and Akela listening to the night noises.

"Hssh! Dogs," he said cheerfully. "The dholes will come down-stream. If ye be not afraid ye can kill them in the shallows."

"When come they?" said Phao. "And where is my Man-cub?" said Akela.

"They come when they come," said Kaa. "Wait and see. As for *thy* Man-cub, from whom thou hast taken a Word and so laid him open to Death, *thy* Man-cub is with *me*, and if he be not already dead the fault is none of thine, bleached dog! Wait here for the dhole, and be glad that the Man-cub and I strike on thy side."

Kaa flashed up-stream again, and moored himself in the middle of the gorge, looking upward at the line of the cliff. Presently he saw Mowgli's head move against the stars, and then there was a whizz in the air, the keen, clean schloop of a body falling feet first, and next minute the boy was at rest again in the loop of Kaa's body.

"It is no leap by night," said Mowgli quietly. "I have jumped twice as far for sport; but that is an evil place above — low bushes and gullies that go down very deep, all full of the Little People. I have put big stones one above the other by the side of three gullies. These I shall throw down with my feet in running, and the Little People will rise up behind me, very angry."

"That is Man's talk and Man's cunning," said Kaa. "Thou art wise, but the Little People are always angry."

"Nay, at twilight all wings near and far rest for a while. I will play with the dhole at twilight, for the dhole hunts best by day. He follows now Won-tolla's blood-trail."

"Chil does not leave a dead ox, nor the dhole the blood-trail," said Kaa.

"Then I will make him a new blood-trail, of his own blood, if I can, and give him dirt to eat. Thou wilt stay here, Kaa, till I come again with my dholes?"

"Aye, but what if they kill thee in the Jungle, or the Little People kill thee before thou canst leap down to the river?"

"When tomorrow comes we will kill for tomorrow," said Mowgli, quoting a Jungle saying; and again, "When I am dead it is time to sing the Death Song. Good hunting, Kaa!"

He loosed his arm from the python's neck and went down the gorge like a log in a freshet, paddling toward the far bank, where he found slack-water, and laughing aloud from sheer happiness. There was nothing Mowgli liked better than, as he himself said, "to pull the whiskers of Death," and make the Jungle know that he was their overlord. He had often, with Baloo's help, robbed bees' nests in single trees, and he knew that the Little People hated the smell of wild garlic. So he gathered a small bundle of it, tied it up with a bark string, and then followed Won-tolla's blood-trail, as it ran southerly from the Lairs, for some five miles, looking at the trees with his head on one side, and chuckling as he looked.

"Mowgli the Frog have I been," said he to himself; "Mowgli the Wolf have I said that I am. Now Mowgli the Ape must I be before I am Mowgli the Buck. At the end I shall be Mowgli the Man. Ho!" and he slid his thumb along the eighteen-inch blade of his knife.

Won-tolla's trail, all rank with dark blood-spots, ran under a forest of thick trees that grew close together and stretched away northeastward, gradually growing thinner and thinner to within two miles of the Bee Rocks. From the last tree to the low scrub of the Bee Rocks was open country, where there was hardly cover enough to hide a wolf. Mowgli trotted along under the trees, judging distances between branch and branch, occasionally climbing up a trunk and taking a trial leap from one tree to another till he came to the open ground, which he studied very carefully for an hour. Then he turned, picked up Won-tolla's trail where he had left it, settled himself in a tree with an outrunning branch some eight feet from the ground, and sat still, sharpening his knife on the sole of his foot and singing to himself.

A little before mid-day, when the sun was very warm, he heard the patter of feet and smelt the abominable smell of the dhole-pack as they trotted pitilessly along Won-tolla's trail. Seen from above, the red dhole does not look half the size of a wolf, but Mowgli knew how strong his feet and jaws were. He watched the sharp bay head of the leader snuffing along the trail, and gave him "Good hunting!"

The brute looked up, and his companions halted behind him, scores and scores of red dogs with low-hung tails, heavy shoulders, weak quarters, and bloody mouths. The dholes are a very silent people as a rule, and they have no manners even in their own Jungle. Fully two hundred must have gathered below him, but he could see that the leaders sniffed hungrily on Won-tolla's trail, and tried to drag the Pack forward. That would never do, or they would be at the Lairs in broad daylight, and Mowgli meant to hold them under his tree till dusk.

"By whose leave do ye come here?" said Mowgli.

"All Jungles are our Jungle," was the reply, and the dhole that gave it bared his white teeth. Mowgli looked down with a smile, and imitated perfectly the sharp chitter-chatter of Chikai, the leaping rat of the Dekkan, meaning the dholes to understand that he considered them no better than Chikai. The Pack closed up round the tree-trunk and the leader bayed savagely, calling Mowgli a tree-ape. For an answer Mowgli stretched down one naked leg and wriggled his bare toes just above the leader's head. That was enough, and more than enough, to wake the Pack to stupid rage. Those who have hair between their toes do not care to be reminded of it. Mowgli caught his foot away as the leader leaped up, and said sweetly: "Dog, red dog! Go back to the Dekkan and eat lizards. Go to Chikai thy brother — dog, dog — red, red dog! There is hair between every toe!" He twiddled his toes a second time.

"Come down ere we starve thee out, hairless ape!" yelled the Pack, and this was exactly what Mowgli wanted. He laid himself down along the branch, his cheek to the bark, his right arm free, and there he told the Pack what he thought and knew about them, their manners, their customs, their mates, and their puppies. There is no speech in the world so rancorous and so stinging as the language the Jungle People use to show scorn and contempt. When you come to think of it you will see how this must be so. As Mowgli told Kaa, he had many little thorns under his tongue, and slowly and deliberately he drove the dholes from silence to growls, from growls to yells, and from yells to hoarse slavery ravings. They tried to answer his taunts, but a cub might as well have tried to answer Kaa in a rage; and all the while Mowgli's right hand lay crooked at his side, ready for action, his feet locked round the branch. The big bay leader had leaped many times in the air, but Mowgli dared not risk a false blow. At last, made furious beyond his natural strength, he bounded up seven or eight feet clear of the ground. Then Mowgli's hand shot out like the head of a tree-snake, and gripped him by the scruff of his neck, and the branch shook with the jar as his weight fell back, almost wrenching Mowgli to the ground. But he never loosed his grip, and inch by inch he hauled the beast, hanging like a drowned jackal, up on the branch. With his left hand he reached for his knife and cut off the red, bushy tail, flinging the dhole back to earth again. That was all he needed. The Pack would not go forward on Won-tolla's trail now till they had killed Mowgli or Mowgli had killed them. He saw them settle down in circles with a quiver of the haunches that meant they were going to stay, and so he climbed to a higher crotch, settled his back comfortably, and went to sleep.

After three or four hours he waked and counted the Pack. They were all there, silent, husky, and dry, with eyes of steel. The sun was beginning to sink. In half an hour the Little People of the Rocks would be ending their labors, and, as you know, the dhole does not fight best in the twilight.

"I did not need such faithful watchers," he said politely, standing up on a branch, "but I will remember this. Ye be true dholes, but to my thinking over much of one kind. For that reason I do not give the big lizard-eater his tail again. Art thou not pleased, Red Dog?"

"I myself will tear out thy stomach!" yelled the leader, scratching at the foot of the tree.

"Nay, but consider, wise rat of the Dekkan. There will now be many litters of little tailless red dogs, yea, with raw red stumps that sting when the sand is hot. Go home, Red Dog, and cry that an ape has done this. Ye will not go? Come, then, with me, and I will make you very wise!"

He moved, Bandar-log fashion, into the next tree, and so on into the next and the next, the Pack following with lifted hungry heads. Now and then he would pretend to fall, and the Pack would tumble one over the other in their haste to be at the death. It was a curious sight — the boy with the knife that shone in the low sunlight as it sifted through the upper branches, and the silent Pack with their red coats all aflame, huddling and following below. When he came to the last tree he took the garlic and rubbed himself all over carefully, and the dholes yelled with scorn. "Ape with a wolf's tongue, dost thou think to cover thy scent?" they said. "We follow to the death."

"Take thy tail," said Mowgli, flinging it back along the course he had taken. The Pack instinctively rushed after it. "And follow now — to the death."

He had slipped down the tree-trunk, and headed like the wind in bare feet for the Bee Rocks, before the dholes saw what he would do.

They gave one deep howl, and settled down to the long, lobbing canter that can at the last run down anything that runs. Mowgli knew their pack-pace to be much slower than that of the wolves, or he would never have risked a two-mile run in full sight. They were sure that the boy was theirs at last, and he was sure that he held them to play with as he pleased. All his trouble was to keep them sufficiently hot behind him to prevent their turning off too soon. He ran cleanly, evenly, and springily; the tailless leader not five yards behind him; and the Pack tailing out over perhaps a quarter of a mile of ground, crazy and blind with the rage of slaughter. So he kept his distance by ear, reserving his last effort for the rush across the Bee Rocks.

The Little People had gone to sleep in the early twilight, for it was not the season of late blossoming flowers; but as Mowgli's first foot-falls rang hollow on the hollow ground he heard a sound as though all the earth were humming. Then he ran as he had never run in his life before, spurned aside one — two — three of the piles of stones into the dark, sweet-smelling gullies; heard a roar like the roar of the sea in a cave; saw with the tail of his eye the air grow dark behind him; saw the current of the Waingunga far below, and a flat, diamond-shaped head in the water; leaped outward with all his strength, the tailless dhole snapping at his shoulder in mid-air, and dropped feet first to the safety of the river, breathless and triumphant. There was not a sting upon him, for the smell of the garlic had checked the Little People for just the few seconds that he was among them. When he rose Kaa's coils were steadying him and things were bounding over the edge of the cliff — great lumps, it seemed, of clustered bees falling like plummets; but before any lump touched water the bees flew upward and the body of a dhole whirled down-stream. Overhead they could hear furious short yells that were drowned in a roar like breakers — the roar of the wings of the Little People of the Rocks. Some of the dholes, too, had fallen into the gullies that communicated with the underground caves, and there choked and fought and snapped among the tumbled honeycombs, and at last, borne up, even when they were dead, on the heaving waves of bees beneath them, shot out of some hole in the river-face, to roll over on the black rubbish-heaps. There were dholes who had leaped short into the trees on the cliffs, and the bees blotted out their shapes; but the greater number of them, maddened by the stings, had flung themselves into the river; and, as Kaa said, the Waingunga was hungry water.

Kaa held Mowgli fast till the boy had recovered his breath.

"We may not stay here," he said. "The Little People are roused indeed. Come!"

Swimming low and diving as often as he could, Mowgli went down the river, knife in hand.

"Slowly, slowly," said Kaa. "One tooth does not kill a hundred unless it be a cobra's, and many of the dholes took water swiftly when they saw the Little People rise."

"The more work for my knife, then. Phai! How the, Little People follow!" Mowgli sank again. The face of the water was blanketed with wild bees, buzzing sullenly and stinging all they found.

"Nothing was ever yet lost by silence," said Kaa — no sting could penetrate his scales — "and thou hast all the long night for the hunting. Hear them howl!"

Nearly half the pack had seen the trap their fellows rushed into, and turning sharp aside had flung themselves into the water where the gorge broke down in steep banks. Their cries of rage and their threats against the "tree-ape" who had brought them to their shame mixed with the yells and growls of those who had been punished by the Little People. To remain ashore was death, and every dhole knew it. Their pack was swept along the current, down to the deep eddies of the Peace Pool, but even there the angry Little People followed and forced them to the water again. Mowgli could hear the voice of the tailless leader bidding his people hold on and kill out every wolf in Seeonee. But he did not waste his time in listening.

"One kills in the dark behind us!" snapped a dhole. "Here is tainted water!"

Mowgli had dived forward like an otter, twitched a struggling dhole under water before he could open his mouth, and dark rings rose as the body plopped up, turning on its side. The dholes tried to turn, but the current prevented them, and the Little People darted at the heads and ears, and they could hear the challenge of the Seeonee Pack growing louder and deeper in the gathering darkness. Again Mowgli dived, and again a dhole went under, and rose dead, and again the clamor broke out at the rear of the pack; some howling that it was best to go ashore, others calling on their leader to lead them back to the Dekkan, and others bidding Mowgli show himself and he killed.

"They come to the fight with two stomachs and several voices," said Kaa. "The rest is with thy brethren below yonder, The Little People go back to sleep. They have chased us far. Now I, too, turn back, for I am not of one skin with any wolf. Good hunting, Little Brother, and remember the dhole bites low."

A wolf came running along the bank on three legs, leaping up and down, laying his head sideways close to the ground, hunching his back, and breaking high into the air, as though he were playing with his cubs. It was Won-tolla, the Outlier, and he said never a word, but continued his horrible sport beside the dholes. They had been long in the water now, and were swimming wearily, their coats drenched and heavy, their bushy tails dragging like sponges, so tired and shaken that they, too, were silent, watching the pair of blazing eyes that moved abreast.

"This is no good hunting," said one, panting.

"Good hunting!" said Mowgli, as he rose boldly at the brute's side, and sent the long knife home behind the shoulder, pushing hard to avoid his dying snap.

"Art thou there, Man-cub?" said Won-tolla across the water.

"Ask of the dead, Outlier," Mowgli replied. "Have none come down-stream? I have filled these dogs' mouths with dirt; I have tricked them in the broad daylight, and their leader lacks his tail, but here be some few for thee still. Whither shall I drive them?"

"I will wait," said Won-tolla. "The night is before me."

Nearer and nearer came the bay of the Seeonee wolves. "For the Pack, for the Full Pack it is met!" and a bend in the river drove the dholes forward among the sands and shoals opposite the Lairs.

Then they saw their mistake. They should have landed half a mile higher up, and rushed the wolves on dry ground. Now it was too late. The bank was lined with burning eyes, and except for the horrible pheeal that had never stopped since sundown, there was no sound in the Jungle. It seemed as though Won-tolla were fawning on them to come ashore; and "Turn and take hold!" said the leader of the dholes. The entire Pack flung themselves at the shore, threshing and squattering through the shoal water, till the face of the Waingunga was all white and torn, and the great ripples went from side to side, like bow-waves from a boat. Mowgli followed the rush, stabbing and slicing as the dholes, huddled together, rushed up the river-beach in one wave.

Then the long fight began, heaving and straining and splitting and scattering and narrowing and broadening along the red, wet sands, and over and between the tangled tree-roots, and through and among the bushes, and in and out of the grass clumps; for even now the dholes were two to one. But they met wolves fighting for all that made the Pack, and not only the short, high, deep-chested, white-tusked hunters of the Pack, but the anxious-eyed lahinis — the she-wolves of the lair, as the saying is — fighting for their litters, with here and there a yearling wolf, his first coat still half woolly, tugging and grappling by their sides. A wolf, you must know, flies at the throat or snaps at the flank, while a dhole, by preference, bites at the belly; so when the dholes were struggling out of the water and had to raise their heads, the odds were with the wolves. On dry land the wolves suffered; but in the water or ashore, Mowgli's knife came and went without ceasing. The Four had worried their way to his side. Gray Brother, crouched between the boy's knees, was protecting his stomach, while the others guarded his back and either side, or stood over him when the shock of a leaping, yelling dhole who had thrown himself full on the steady blade bore him down. For the rest, it was one tangled confusion — a locked and swaying mob that moved from right to left and from left to right along the bank; and also ground round and round slowly on its own center. Here would be a heaving mound, like a water-blister in a whirlpool, which would break like a water-blister, and throw up four or five mangled dogs, each striving to get back to the center; here would be a single wolf borne down by two or three dholes, laboriously dragging them forward, and sinking the while; here a yearling cub would he held up by the pressure round him, though he had been killed early, while his mother, crazed with dumb rage, rolled over and over, snapping, and passing on; and in the middle of the thickest press, perhaps, one wolf and one dhole, forgetting everything else, would be manoeuvring for first hold till they were whirled away by a rush of furious fighters. Once Mowgli passed Akela, a dhole on either flank, and his all but toothless jaws closed over the loins of a third; and once he saw Phao, his teeth set in the throat of a dhole, tugging the unwilling beast forward till the yearlings could finish him. But the bulk of the fight was blind flurry and smother in the dark; hit, trip, and tumble, yelp, groan, and worry-worry-worry, round him and behind him and above him. As the night wore on, the quick, giddy-go-round motion increased. The dholes were cowed and afraid to attack the stronger wolves, but did not yet dare to run away. Mowgli felt that the end was coming soon, and contented himself with striking merely to cripple. The yearlings were growing bolder; there was time now and again to breathe, and pass a word to a friend, and the mere flicker of the knife would sometimes turn a dog aside.

"The meat is very near the bone," Gray Brother yelled. He was bleeding from a score of flesh-wounds.

"But the bone is yet to he cracked," said Mowgli. "Eowawa! *Thus* do we do in the Jungle!" The red blade ran like a flame along the side of a dhole whose hind-quarters were hidden by the weight of a clinging wolf.

"My kill!" snorted the wolf through his wrinkled nostrils. "Leave him to me."

"Is thy stomach still empty, Outlier?" said Mowgli. Won-tolla was fearfully punished, but his grip had paralyzed the dhole, who could not turn round and reach him.

"By the Bull that bought me," said Mowgli, with a bitter laugh, "it is the tailless one!" And indeed it was the big bay-colored leader.

"It is not wise to kill cubs and lahinis," Mowgli went on philosophically, wiping the blood out of his eyes, "unless one has also killed the Outlier; and it is in my stomach that this Won-tolla kills thee."

A dhole leaped to his leader's aid; but before his teeth had found Won-tolla's flank, Mowgli's knife was in his throat, and Gray Brother took what was left.

"And thus do we do in the Jungle," said Mowgli.

Won-tolla said not a word, only his jaws were closing and closing on the backbone as his life ebbed. The dhole shuddered, his head dropped, and he lay still, and Won-tolla dropped above him.

"Huh! The Blood Debt is paid," said Mowgli. "Sing the song, Won-tolla."

"He hunts no more," said Gray Brother; "and Akela, too, is silent this long time."

"The bone is cracked!" thundered Phao, son of Phaona. "They go! Kill, kill out, O hunters of the Free

People!"

Dhole after dhole was slinking away from those dark and bloody sands to the river, to the thick Jungle, up-stream or down-stream as he saw the road clear.

"The debt! The debt!" shouted Mowgli. "Pay the debt! They have slain the Lone Wolf! Let not a dog go!"

He was flying to the river, knife in hand, to check any dhole who dared to take water, when, from under a mound of nine dead, rose Akela's head and fore-quarters, and Mowgli dropped on his knees beside the Lone Wolf.

"Said I not it would be my last fight?" Akela gasped. "It is good hunting. And thou, Little Brother?"

"I live, having killed many."

"Even so. I die, and I would — I would die by thee, Little Brother."

Mowgli took the terrible scarred head on his knees, and put his arms round the torn neck.

"It is long since the old days of Shere Khan, and a Man-cub that rolled naked in the dust."

"Nay, nay, I am a wolf. I am of one skin with the Free People," Mowgli cried. "It is no will of mine that I am a man."

"Thou art a man, Little Brother, wolfling of my watching. Thou art a man, or else the Pack had fled before the dhole. My life I owe to thee, and today thou hast saved the Pack even as once I saved thee. Hast thou forgotten? All debts are paid now. Go to thine own people. I tell thee again, eye of my eye, this hunting is ended. Go to thine own people."

"I will never go. I will hunt alone in the Jungle. I have said it."

"After the summer come the Rains, and after the Rains comes the spring. Go back before thou art driven."

"Who will drive me?"

"Mowgli will drive Mowgli. Go back to thy people. Go to Man."

"When Mowgli drives Mowgli I will go," Mowgli answered.

"There is no more to say," said Akela. "Little Brother, canst thou raise me to my feet? I also was a leader of the Free People."

Very carefully and gently Mowgli lifted the bodies aside, and raised Akela to his feet, both arms round him, and the Lone Wolf drew a long breath, and began the Death Song that a leader of the Pack should sing when he dies. It gathered strength as he went on, lifting and lifting, and ringing far across the river, till it came to the last "Good hunting!" and Akela shook himself clear of Mowgli for an instant, and, leaping into the air, fell backward dead upon his last and most terrible kill.

Mowgli sat with his head on his knees, careless of anything else, while the remnant of the flying dholes were being overtaken and run down by the merciless lahinis. Little by little the cries died away, and the wolves returned limping, as their wounds stiffened, to take stock of the losses. Fifteen of the Pack, as well as half a dozen lahinis, lay dead by the river, and of the others not one was unmarked. And Mowgli sat through it all till the cold daybreak, when Phao's wet, red muzzle was dropped in his hand, and Mowgli drew back to show the gaunt body of Akela.

"Good hunting!" said Phao, as though Akela were still alive, and then over his bitten shoulder to the others: "Howl, dogs! A Wolf has died tonight!"

But of all the Pack of two hundred fighting dholes, whose boast was that all jungles were their Jungle, and that no living thing could stand before them, not one returned to the Dekkan to carry that word.

Chil's Song

[This is the song that Chil sang as the kites dropped down one after another to the river-bed, when the great fight was finished. Chil is good friends with everybody, but he is a cold-blooded kind of creature at heart, because he knows that almost everybody in the Jungle comes to him in the long-run.]

These were my companions going forth by night —
    (For Chil! Look you, for Chil!)
Now come I to whistle them the ending of the fight.
    (Chil! Vanguards of Chil!}
Word they gave me overhead of quarry newly slain,
Word I gave them underfoot of buck upon the plain.
Here's an end of every trail — they shall not speak
    again!

They that called the hunting-cry — they that
    followed fast —
    (For Chil! Look you, for Chil!)
They that bade the sambhur wheel, or pinned him
    as he passed —
    (Chil! Vanguards of Chil!)
They that lagged behind the scent — they that ran
    before,

They that shunned the level horn — they that
      overbore.
Here's an end of every trail — they shall not follow
      more.
These were my companions. Pity 'twas they died!
      (For Chil! Look you, for Chil!)
Now come I to comfort them that knew them in
      their pride.
      (Chil! Vanguards of Chil!)
Tattered flank and sunken eye, open mouth and red,
Locked and lank and lone they lie, the dead upon
      their dead.
Here's an end of every trail — and here my hosts are
      fed.

The Spring Running

Man goes to Man! Cry the challenge through the
    Jungle!
He that was our Brother goes away.
Hear, now, and judge, O ye People of the Jungle, —
    Answer, who shall turn him — who shall stay?

Man goes to Man! He is weeping in the Jungle:
    He that was our Brother sorrows sore!
Man goes to Man! (Oh, we loved him in the Jungle!)
    To the Man-Trail where we may not follow more.

*T*he second year after the great fight with Red Dog
and the death of Akela, Mowgli must have been nearly
seventeen years old. He looked older, for hard exercise,
the best of good eating, and baths whenever he felt in
the least hot or dusty, had given him strength and
growth far beyond his age. He could swing by one hand
from a top branch for half an hour at a time, when he
had occasion to look along the tree-roads. He could
stop a young buck in mid-gallop and throw him sideways by the head. He could even jerk over the big, blue
wild boars that lived in the Marshes of the North. The

Jungle People who used to fear him for his wits feared
him now for his strength, and when he moved quietly
on his own affairs the mere whisper of his coming
cleared the wood-paths. And yet the look in his eyes
was always gentle. Even when he fought, his eyes never
blazed as Bagheera's did. They only grew more and
more interested and excited; and that was one of the
things that Bagheera himself did not understand.

He asked Mowgli about it, and the boy laughed and
said. "When I miss the kill I am angry. When I must
go empty for two days I am very angry. Do not my
eyes talk then?"

"The mouth is hungry," said Bagheera, "but the eyes
say nothing. Hunting, eating, or swimming, it is all
one — like a stone in wet or dry weather." Mowgli
looked at him lazily from under his long eyelashes,
and, as usual, the panther's head dropped. Bagheera
knew his master.

They were lying out far up the side of a hill over-
looking the Waingunga, and the morning mists hung
below them in bands of white and green. As the sun
rose it changed into bubbling seas of red gold, churned
off, and let the low rays stripe the dried grass on which
Mowgli and Bagheera were resting. It was the end of
the cold weather, the leaves and the trees looked worn
and faded, and there was a dry, ticking rustle every-
where when the wind blew. A little leaf tap-tap-tapped
furiously against a twig, as a single leaf caught in a
current will. It roused Bagheera, for he snuffed the
morning air with a deep, hollow cough, threw himself
on his back, and struck with his fore-paws at the
nodding leaf above.

"The year turns," he said. "The Jungle goes forward.
The Time of New Talk is near. That leaf knows. It is
very good."

"The grass is dry," Mowgli answered, pulling up a

tuft. "Even Eye-of-the-Spring [that is a little trumpet-shaped, waxy red flower that runs in and out among the grasses] — even Eye-of-the Spring is shut, and . . . Bagheera, *is* it well for the Black Panther so to lie on his back and beat with his paws in the air, as though he were the tree-cat?"

"Aowh?" said Bagheera. He seemed to be thinking of other things.

"I say, *is* it well for the Black Panther so to mouth and cough, and howl and roll? Remember, we be the Masters of the Jungle, thou and I."

"Indeed, yes; I hear, Man-cub." Bagheera rolled over hurriedly and sat up, the dust on his ragged black flanks. (He was just casting his winter coat.) "We be surely the Masters of the Jungle! Who is so strong as Mowgli? Who so wise?" There was a curious drawl in the voice that made Mowgli turn to see whether by any chance the Black Panther were making fun of him, for the Jungle is full of words that sound like one thing, but mean another. "I said we be beyond question the Masters of the Jungle," Bagheera repeated. "Have I done wrong? I did not know that the Man-cub no longer lay upon the ground. Does he fly, then?"

Mowgli sat with his elbows on his knees, looking out across the valley at the daylight. Somewhere down in the woods below a bird was trying over in a husky, reedy voice the first few notes of his spring song. It was no more than a shadow of the liquid, tumbling call he would be pouring later, but Bagheera heard it.

"I said the Time of New Talk is near," growled the panther, switching his tail.

"I hear," Mowgli answered. "Bagheera, why dost thou shake all over? The sun is warm."

"That is Ferao, the scarlet woodpecker," said Bagheera. "*He* has not forgotten. Now I, too, must remember my song," and he began purring and crooning to himself, harking back dissatisfied again and again.

"There is no game afoot," said Mowgli.

"Little Brother, are *both* thine ears stopped? That is no killing-word, but my song that I make ready against the need."

"I had forgotten. I shall know when the Time of New Talk is here, because then thou and the others all run away and leave me alone." Mowgli spoke rather savagely.

"But, indeed, Little Brother," Bagheera began, "we do not always —"

"I say ye do," said Mowgli, shooting out his forefinger angrily. "Ye *do* run away, and I, who am the Master of the Jungle, must needs walk alone. How was it last season, when I would gather sugar-cane from the fields of a Man-Pack? I sent a runner — I sent thee! — to Hathi, bidding him to come upon such a night and pluck the sweet grass for me with his trunk."

"He came only two nights later," said Bagheera, cowering a little; "and of that long, sweet grass that pleased thee so he gathered more than any Man-cub could eat in all the nights of the Rains. That was no fault of mine."

"He did not come upon the night when I sent him the word. No, he was trumpeting and running and roaring through the valleys in the moonlight. His trail was like the trail of three elephants, for he would not hide among the trees. He danced in the moonlight before the houses of the Man-Pack. I saw him, and yet he would not come to me; and *I* am the Master of the Jungle!"

"It was the Time of New Talk," said the panther, always very humble. "Perhaps, Little Brother, thou didst not that time call him by a Master-word? Listen to Ferao, and be glad!"

Mowgli's bad temper seemed to have boiled itself
away. He lay back with his head on his arms, his eyes
shut. "I do not know — nor do I care," he said sleepily.
"Let us sleep, Bagheera. My stomach is heavy in me.
Make me a rest for my head."

The panther lay down again with a sigh, because he
could hear Ferao practising and repractising his song
against the Springtime of New Talk, as they say.

In an Indian Jungle the seasons slide one into the
other almost without division. There seem to be only
two — the wet and the dry; but if you look closely below
the torrents of rain and the clouds of char and dust
you will find all four going round in their regular ring.
Spring is the most wonderful, because she has not to
cover a clean, bare field with new leaves and flowers,
but to drive before her and to put away the hanging-on,
oversurviving raffle of half-green things which the
gentle winter has suffered to live, and to make the
partly-dressed stale earth feel new and young once
more. And this she does so well that there is no spring
in the world like the Jungle spring.

There is one day when all things are tired, and the
very smells, as they drift on the heavy air, are old and
used. One cannot explain this, but it feels so. Then
there is another day — to the eye nothing whatever has
changed — when all the smells are new and delightful,
and the whiskers of the Jungle People quiver to their
roots, and the winter hair comes away from their sides
in long, draggled locks. Then, perhaps, a little rain falls,
and all the trees and the bushes and the bamboos and
the mosses and the juicy-leaved plants wake with a
noise of growing that you can almost hear, and under
this noise runs, day and night, a deep hum. *that* is the
noise of the spring — a vibrating boom which is neither
bees, nor falling water, nor the wind in tree-tops, but
the purring of the warm, happy world.

Up to this year Mowgli had always delighted in the turn of the seasons. It was he who generally saw the first Eye-of-the-Spring deep down among the grasses, and the first bank of spring clouds, which are like nothing else in the Jungle. His voice could be heard in all sorts of wet, star-lighted, blossoming places, helping the big frogs through their choruses, or mocking the little upside-down owls that hoot through the white nights. Like all his people, spring was the season he chose for his flittings — moving, for the mere joy of rushing through the warm air, thirty, forty, or fifty miles between twilight and the morning star, and coming back panting and laughing and wreathed with strange flowers. The Four did not follow him on these wild ringings of the Jungle, but went off to sing songs with other wolves. The Jungle People are very busy in the spring, and Mowgli could hear them grunting and screaming and whistling according to their kind. Their voices then are different from their voices at other times of the year, and that is one of the reasons why spring in the Jungle is called the Time of New Talk.

But that spring, as he told Bagheera, his stomach was changed in him. Ever since the bamboo shoots turned spotty-brown he had been looking forward to the morning when the smells should change. But when the morning came, and Mor the Peacock, blazing in bronze and blue and gold, cried it aloud all along the misty woods, and Mowgli opened his mouth to send on the cry, the words choked between his teeth, and a feeling came over him that began at his toes and ended in his hair — a feeling of pure unhappiness, so that he looked himself over to be sure that he had not trod on a thorn. Mor cried the new smells, the other birds took it over, and from the rocks by the Waingunga he heard Bagheera's hoarse scream — something between the scream of an eagle and the neighing of a horse. There was a yelling and scattering of Bandar-log in the new-budding branches above, and there stood Mowgli, his chest, filled to answer Mor, sinking in little gasps as the breath was driven out of it by this unhappiness.

He stared all round him, but he could see no more than the mocking Bandar-log scudding through the trees, and Mor, his tail spread in full splendor, dancing on the slopes below.

"The smells have changed," screamed Mor. "Good hunting, Little Brother! Where is thy answer?"

"Little Brother, good hunting!" whistled Chil the Kite and his mate, swooping down together. The two baffed under Mowgli's nose so close that a pinch of downy white feathers brushed away.

A light spring rain — elephant-rain they call it — drove across the Jungle in a belt half a mile wide, left the new leaves wet and nodding behind, and died out in a double rainbow and a light roll of thunder. The spring hum broke out for a minute, and was silent, but all the Jungle Folk seemed to be giving tongue at once. All except Mowgli.

"I have eaten good food," he said to himself. "I have drunk good water. Nor does my throat burn and grow small, as it did when I bit the blue-spotted root that Oo the Turtle said was clean food. But my stomach is heavy, and I have given very bad talk to Bagheera and others, people of the Jungle and my people. Now, too, I am hot and now I am cold, and now I am neither hot nor cold, but angry with that which I cannot see. Huhu! It is time to make a running! Tonight I will cross the ranges; yes, I will make a spring running to the Marshes of the North, and back again. I have hunted too easily too long. The Four shall come with me, for they grow as fat as white grubs."

He called, but never one of the Four answered. They were far beyond earshot, singing over the spring songs

— the Moon and Sambhur Songs — with the wolves of the pack; for in the spring-time the Jungle People make very little difference between the day and the night. He gave the sharp, barking note, but his only answer was the mocking maiou of the little spotted tree-cat winding in and out among the branches for early birds' nests. At this he shook all over with rage, and half drew his knife. Then he became very haughty, though there was no one to see him, and stalked severely down the hillside, chin up and eyebrows down. But never a single one of his people asked him a question, for they were all too busy with their own affairs.

"Yes," said Mowgli to himself, though in his heart he knew that he had no reason. "Let the Red Dhole come from the Dekkan, or the Red Flower dance among the bamboos, and all the Jungle runs whining to Mowgli, calling him great elephant-names. But now, because Eye-of-the-Spring is red, and Mor, forsooth, must show his naked legs in some spring dance, the Jungle goes mad as Tabaqui. . . . By the Bull that bought me! am I the Master of the Jungle, or am I not? Be silent! What do ye here?"

A couple of young wolves of the Pack were cantering down a path, looking for open ground in which to fight. (You will remember that the Law of the Jungle forbids fighting where the Pack can see.) Their neck-bristles were as stiff as wire, and they bayed furiously, crouching for the first grapple. Mowgli leaped forward, caught one outstretched throat in either hand, expecting to fling the creatures backward as he had often done in games or Pack hunts. But he had never before interfered with a spring fight. The two leaped forward and dashed him aside, and without word to waste rolled over and over close locked.

Mowgli was on his feet almost before he fell, his knife and his white teeth were bared, and at that minute he would have killed both for no reason but that they were fighting when he wished them to be quiet, although every wolf has full right under the Law to fight. He danced round them with lowered shoulders and quivering hand, ready to send in a double blow when the first flurry of the scuffle should be over; but while he waited the strength seemed to ebb from his body, the knife-point lowered, and he sheathed the knife and watched.

"I have surely eaten poison," he sighed at last. "Since I broke up the Council with the Red Flower — since I killed Shere Khan — none of the Pack could fling me aside. And these be only tail-wolves in the Pack, little hunters! My strength is gone from me, and presently I shall die. Oh, Mowgli, why dost thou not kill them both?"

The fight went on till one wolf ran away, and Mowgli was left alone on the torn and bloody ground, looking now at his knife, and now at his legs and arms, while the feeling of unhappiness he had never known before covered him as water covers a log.

He killed early that evening and ate but little, so as to be in good fettle for his spring running, and he ate alone because all the Jungle People were away singing or fighting. It was a perfect white night, as they call it. All green things seemed to have made a month's growth since the morning. The branch that was yellow-leaved the day before dripped sap when Mowgli broke it. The mosses curled deep and warm over his feet, the young grass had no cutting edges, and all the voices of the Jungle boomed like one deep harp-string touched by the moon — the Moon of New Talk, who splashed her light full on rock and pool, slipped it between trunk and creeper, and sifted it through a million leaves. Forgetting his unhappiness, Mowgli sang aloud with pure delight as he settled into his stride. It was more like flying than anything else, for he had chosen the long downward slope that leads to the Northern Marshes through the heart of the main Jungle, where the springy ground deadened the fall of his feet. A man-taught man would have picked his way with many stumbles through the cheating moonlight, but Mowgli's muscles, trained by years of experience, bore him up as though he were a feather. When a rotten log or a hidden stone turned under his foot he saved himself, never checking his pace, without effort and without thought. When he tired of ground-going he threw up his hands monkey-fashion to the nearest creeper, and seemed to float rather than to climb up into the thin branches, whence he would follow a tree-road till his mood changed, and he shot downward in a long, leafy curve to the levels again. There were still, hot hollows surrounded by wet rocks where he could hardly breathe for the heavy scents of the night flowers and the bloom along the creeper buds; dark avenues where the moonlight lay in belts as regular as checkered marbles in a church aisle; thickets where the wet young growth stood breast-high about him and threw its arms round his waist; and hilltops crowned with broken rock, where he leaped from stone to stone above the lairs of the frightened little foxes. He would hear, very faint and far off, the chug-drug of a boar sharpening his tusks on a bole; and would come across the great gray brute all alone, scribing and rending the bark of a tall tree, his mouth dripping with foam, and his eyes blazing like fire. Or he would turn aside to the sound of clashing horns and hissing grunts, and dash past a couple of furious sambhur, staggering to and fro with lowered heads, striped with blood that showed black in the moonlight. Or at some rushing ford he would hear Jacala the Crocodile bellowing like a bull, or disturb a twined knot of the Poison People, but before they could strike he would be away and across the glistening shingle, and deep in the Jungle again.

So he ran, sometimes shouting, sometimes singing to himself, the happiest thing in all the Jungle that night, till the smell of the flowers warned him that he was near the marshes, and those lay far beyond his farthest hunting-grounds.

Here, again, a man-trained man would have sunk overhead in three strides, but Mowgli's feet had eyes in them, and they passed him from tussock to tussock and clump to quaking clump without asking help from the eyes in his head. He ran out to the middle of the swamp, disturbing the duck as he ran, and sat down on a moss-coated tree-trunk lapped in the black water. The marsh was awake all round him, for in the spring the Bird People sleep very lightly, and companies of them were coming or going the night through. But no one took any notice of Mowgli sitting among the tall reeds humming songs without words, and looking at the soles of his hard brown feet in case of neglected thorns. All his unhappiness seemed to have been left behind in his own Jungle, and he was just beginning a full-throat song when it came back again — ten times worse than before.

This time Mowgli was frightened. "It is here also!" he said half aloud. "It has followed me," and he looked over his shoulder to see whether the It were not standing behind him. "There is no one here." The night noises of the marsh went on, but never a bird or beast spoke to him, and the new feeling of misery grew.

"I have surely eaten poison," he said in an awe-stricken voice. "It must be that carelessly I have eaten poison, and my strength is going from me. I was afraid — and yet it was not *I* that was afraid — Mowgli was afraid when the two wolves fought. Akela, or even Phao, would have silenced them; yet Mowgli was afraid. That is true sign I have eaten poison. . . . But what do they care in the Jungle? They sing and howl and fight, and run in companies under the moon, and I — Hai-mai! — I am dying in the marshes, of that poison which I have eaten." He was so sorry for himself that he nearly wept. "And after," he went on, "they will find me lying in the black water. Nay, I will go back to my own Jungle, and I will die upon the Council Rock, and Bagheera, whom I love, if he is not screaming in the valley — Bagheera, perhaps, may watch by what is left for a little, lest Chil use me as he used Akela."

A large, warm tear splashed down on his knee, and, miserable as he was, Mowgli felt happy that he was so miserable, if you can understand that upside-down sort of happiness. "As Chil the Kite used Akela," he repeated, "on the night I saved the Pack from Red Dog." He was quiet for a little, thinking of the last words of the Lone Wolf, which you, of course, remember. "Now Akela said to me many foolish things before he died, for when we die our stomachs change. He said . . . None the less, I *am* of the Jungle!"

In his excitement, as he remembered the fight on Waingunga bank, he shouted the last words aloud, and a wild buffalo-cow among the reeds sprang to her knees, snorting, "Man!"

"Uhh!" said Mysa the Wild Buffalo (Mowgli could hear him turn in his wallow), "*That* is no man. It is only the hairless wolf of the Seeonee Pack. On such nights runs he to and fro."

"Uhh!" said the cow, dropping her head again to graze, "I thought it was Man."

"I say no. Oh, Mowgli, is it danger?" lowed Mysa.

"Oh, Mowgli, is it danger?" the boy called back mockingly. "That is all Mysa thinks for: Is it danger? But for Mowgli, who goes to and fro in the Jungle by night, watching, what do ye care?"

"How loud he cries!" said the cow. "Thus do they cry," Mysa answered contemptuously, "who, having torn up the grass, know not how to eat it."

"For less than this," Mowgli groaned to himself, "for less than this even last Rains I had pricked Mysa out of his wallow, and ridden him through the swamp on a rush halter." He stretched a hand to break one of the feathery reeds, but drew it back with a sigh. Mysa went on steadily chewing the cud, and the long grass ripped where the cow grazed. "I will not die *here*," he said angrily. "Mysa, who is of one blood with Jacala and the pig, would see me. Let us go beyond the swamp and see what comes. Never have I run such a spring running – hot and cold together. Up, Mowgli!"

He could not resist the temptation of stealing across the reeds to Mysa and pricking him with the point of his knife. The great dripping bull broke out of his wallow like a shell exploding, while Mowgli laughed till he sat down.

"Say now that the hairless wolf of the Seeonee Pack once herded thee, Mysa," he called.

"Wolf! *Thou?*" the bull snorted, stamping in the mud. "All the jungle knows thou wast a herder of tame cattle – such a man's brat as shouts in the dust by the crops yonder. *Thou* of the Jungle! What hunter would have crawled like a snake among the leeches, and for a muddy jest – a jackal's jest – have shamed me before my cow? Come to firm ground, and I will – I will . . ." Mysa frothed at the mouth, for Mysa has nearly the worst temper of anyone in the Jungle.

Mowgli watched him puff and blow with eyes that never changed. When he could make himself heard through the pattering mud, he said: "What Man-Pack lair here by the marshes, Mysa? This is new Jungle to me."

"Go north, then," roared the angry bull, for Mowgli had pricked him rather sharply. "It was a naked cow-herd's jest. Go and tell them at the village at the foot of the marsh."

"The Man-Pack do not love jungle-tales, nor do I think, Mysa, that a scratch more or less on thy hide is any matter for a council. But I will go and look at this village. Yes, I will go. Softly now. It is not every night that the Master of the Jungle comes to herd thee."

He stepped out to the shivering ground on the edge of the marsh, well knowing that Mysa would never charge over it and laughed, as he ran, to think of the bull's anger.

"My strength is not altogether gone," he said. "It may be that the poison is not to the bone. There is a star sitting low yonder." He looked at it between his half-shut hands. "By the Bull that bought me, it is the Red Flower — the Red Flower that I lay beside before — before I came even to the first Seeonee Pack! Now that I have seen, I will finish the running."

The marsh ended in a broad plain where a light twinkled. It was a long time since Mowgli had concerned himself with the doings of men, but this night the glimmer of the Red Flower drew him forward.

"I will look," said he, "as I did in the old days, and I will see how far the Man-Pack has changed."

Forgetting that he was no longer in his own Jungle, where he could do what he pleased, he trod carelessly through the dew-loaded grasses till he came to the hut where the light stood. Three or four yelping dogs gave tongue, for he was on the outskirts of a village.

"Ho!" said Mowgli, sitting down noiselessly, after sending back a deep wolf-growl that silenced the curs. "What comes will come. Mowgli, what hast thou to do anymore with the lairs of the Man-Pack?" He rubbed his mouth, remembering where a stone had struck it years ago when the other Man-Pack had cast him out.

The door of the hut opened, and a woman stood peering out into the darkness. A child cried, and the woman said over her shoulder, "Sleep. It was but a jackal that waked the dogs. In a little time morning comes."

Mowgli in the grass began to shake as though he had fever. He knew that voice well, but to make sure he cried softly, surprised to find how man's talk came back, "Messua! O Messua!"

"Who calls?" said the woman, a quiver in her voice.

"Hast thou forgotten?" said Mowgli. His throat was dry as he spoke.

"If it be *thou,* what name did I give thee? Say!" She had half shut the door, and her hand was clutching at her breast.

"Nathoo! Ohe, Nathoo!" said Mowgli, for, as you remember, that was the name Messua gave him when he first came to the Man-Pack.

"Come, my son," she called, and Mowgli stepped into the light, and looked full at Messua, the woman who had been good to him, and whose life he had saved from the Man-Pack so long before. She was older, and her hair was gray, but her eyes and her voice had not changed. Womanlike, she expected to find Mowgli where she had left him, and her eyes traveled upward in a puzzled way from his chest to his head, that touched the top of the door.

"My son," she stammered; and then, sinking to his feet: "But it is no longer my son. It is a Godling of the Woods! Ahai!"

As he stood in the red light of the oil-lamp, strong, tall, and beautiful, his long black hair sweeping over his shoulders, the knife swinging at his neck, and his head crowned with a wreath of white jasmine, he might easily have been mistaken for some wild god of a jungle legend. The child half asleep on a cot sprang up and shrieked aloud with terror. Messua turned to soothe him, while Mowgli stood still, looking in at the water-jars and the cooking-pots, the grain-bin, and all the other human belongings that he found himself remembering so well.

"What wilt thou eat or drink?" Messua murmured. "This is all thine. We owe our lives to thee. But art thou him I called Nathoo, or a Godling, indeed?"

"I am Nathoo," said Mowgli, "I am very far from my own place. I saw this light, and came hither. I did not know thou wast here."

"After we came to Khanhiwara," Messua said timidly, "the English would have helped us against those villagers that sought to burn us. Rememberest thou?"

"Indeed, I have not forgotten."

"But when the English Law was made ready, we went to the village of those evil people, and it was no more to be found."

"That also I remember," said Mowgli, with a quiver of his nostril.

"My man, therefore, took service in the fields, and at last — for, indeed, he was a strong man — we held a little land here. It is not so rich as the old village, but we do not need much — we two."

"Where is he the man that dug in the dirt when he was afraid on that night?"

"He is dead — a year."

"And he?" Mowgli pointed to the child.

"My son that was born two Rains ago. If thou art a Godling, give him the Favor of the Jungle, that he may be safe among thy — thy people, as we were safe on that night."

She lifted up the child, who, forgetting his fright, reached out to play with the knife that hung on Mowgli's chest, and Mowgli put the little fingers aside very carefully.

"And if thou art Nathoo whom the tiger carried away," Messua went on, choking, "he is then thy younger brother. Give him an elder brother's blessing."

"Hai-mai! What do I know of the thing called a blessing? I am neither a Godling nor his brother, and — O mother, mother, my heart is heavy in me." He shivered as he set down the child.

"Like enough," said Messua, bustling among the cooking-pots. "This comes of running about the marshes by night. Beyond question, the fever had soaked thee to the marrow." Mowgli smiled a little at the idea of anything in the Jungle hurting him. "I will make a fire, and thou shalt drink warm milk. Put away the jasmine wreath: the smell is heavy in so small a place."

Mowgli sat down, muttering, with his face in his hands. All manner of strange feelings that he had never felt before were running over him, exactly as though he had been poisoned, and he felt dizzy and a little sick. He drank the warm milk in long gulps, Messua patting him on the shoulder from time to time, not quite sure whether he were her son Nathoo of the long ago days, or some wonderful Jungle being, but glad to feel that he was at least flesh and blood.

"Son," she said at last, — her eyes were full of pride, — "have any told thee that thou art beautiful beyond all men?"

"Hah?" said Mowgli, for naturally he had never heard anything of the kind. Messua laughed softly and happily. The look in his face was enough for her. "I am the first, then? It is right, though it comes seldom, that a mother should tell her son these good things. Thou art very beautiful. Never have I looked upon such a man."

Mowgli twisted his head and tried to see over his

own hard shoulder, and Messua laughed again so long that Mowgli, not knowing why, was forced to laugh with her, and the child ran from one to the other, laughing too.

"Nay, thou must not mock thy brother," said Messua, catching him to her breast. "When thou art one-half as fair we will marry thee to the youngest daughter of a king, and thou shalt ride great elephants."

Mowgli could not understand one word in three of the talk here; the warm milk was taking effect on him after his long run, so he curled up and in a minute was deep asleep, and Messua put the hair back from his eyes, threw a cloth over him, and was happy. Jungle-fashion, he slept out the rest of that night and all the next day; for his instincts, which never wholly slept, warned him there was nothing to fear. He waked at last with a bound that shook the hut, for the cloth over his face made him dream of traps; and there he stood, his hand on his knife, the sleep all heavy in his rolling eyes, ready for any fight.

Messua laughed, and set the evening meal before him. There were only a few coarse cakes baked over the smoky fire, some rice, and a lump of sour preserved tamarinds — just enough to go on with till he could get to his evening kill. The smell of the dew in the marshes made him hungry and restless. He wanted to finish his spring running, but the child insisted on sitting in his arms, and Messua would have it that his long, blue-black hair must be combed out. So she sang, as she combed, foolish little baby-songs, now calling Mowgli her son, and now begging him to give some of his jungle power to the child. The hut door was closed, but Mowgli heard a sound he knew well, and saw Messua's jaw drop with horror as a great gray paw came under the bottom of the door, and Gray Brother outside whined a muffled and penitent whine of anxiety and fear.

"Out and wait! Ye would not come when I called," said Mowgli in Jungle-talk, without turning his head, and the great gray paw disappeared.

"Do not — do not bring thy — thy servants with thee," said Messua. "I — we have always lived at peace with the Jungle."

"It is peace," said Mowgli, rising. "Think of that night on the road to Khanhiwara. There were scores of such folk before thee and behind thee. But I see that even in springtime the Jungle People do not always forget. Mother, I go."

Messua drew aside humbly — he was indeed a wood-god, she thought; but as his hand was on the door the mother in her made her throw her arms round Mowgli's neck again and again.

"Come back!" she whispered. "Son or no son, come back, for I love thee — Look, he too grieves."

The child was crying because the man with the shiny knife was going away.

"Come back again," Messua repeated. "By night or by day this door is never shut to thee."

Mowgli's throat worked as though the cords in it were being pulled, and his voice seemed to be dragged from it as he answered, "I will surely come back."

"And now," he said, as he put by the head of the fawning wolf on the threshold, "I have a little cry against thee, Gray Brother. Why came ye not all four when I called so long ago?"

"So long ago? It was but last night. I — we — were singing in the Jungle the new songs, for this is the Time of New Talk. Rememberest thou?"

"Truly, truly."

"And as soon as the songs were sung," Gray Brother went on earnestly, "I followed thy trail. I ran from all the others and followed hot-foot. But, O Little Brother, what hast *thou* done, eating and sleeping with the Man-Pack?"

"If ye had come when I called, this had never been," said Mowgli, running much faster.

"And now what is to be?" said Gray Brother. Mowgli was going to answer when a girl in a white cloth came down some path that led from the outskirts of the village. Gray Brother dropped out of sight at once, and Mowgli backed noiselessly into a field of high-springing crops. He could almost have touched her with his hand when the warm, green stalks closed before his face and he disappeared like a ghost. The girl screamed, for she thought she had seen a spirit, and then she gave a deep sigh. Mowgli parted the stalks with his hands and watched her till she was out of sight.

"And now I do not know," he said, sighing in his turn. "*Why* did ye not come when I called?"

"We follow thee — we follow thee," Gray Brother mumbled, licking at Mowgli's heel. "We follow thee always, except in the Time of the New Talk."

"And would ye follow me to the Man-Pack?" Mowgli whispered.

"Did I not follow thee on the night our old Pack cast thee out? Who waked thee lying among the crops?"

"Aye, but again?"

"Have I not followed thee tonight?"

"Aye, but again and again, and it may be again, Gray Brother?"

Gray Brother was silent. When he spoke he growled to himself, "The Black One spoke truth."

"And he said?"

"Man goes to Man at the last. Raksha, our mother, said —"

"So also said Akela on the night of Red Dog," Mowgli muttered.

"So also says Kaa, who is wiser than us all."

"What dost thou say, Gray Brother?"

"They cast thee out once, with bad talk. They cut thy mouth with stones. They sent Buldeo to slay thee. They would have thrown thee into the Red Flower. Thou, and not I, hast said that they are evil and senseless. Thou, and not I — I follow my own people — didst let in the Jungle upon them. Thou, and not I, didst make song against them more bitter even than our song against Red Dog."

"I ask thee what *thou* sayest?"

They were talking as they ran. Gray Brother cantered on a while without replying, and then he said, — between bound and bound as it were, — "Man-cub — Master of the Jungle — Son of Raksha, Lair-brother to me — though I forget for a little while in the spring, thy trail is my trail, thy lair is my lair, thy kill is my kill, and thy death-fight is my death-fight. I speak for the Three. But what wilt thou say to the Jungle?"

"That is well thought. Between the sight and the kill it is not good to wait. Go before and cry them all to the Council Rock, and I will tell them what is in my stomach. But they may not come — in the Time of New Talk they may forget me."

"Hast thou, then, forgotten nothing?" snapped Gray Brother over his shoulder, as he laid himself down to gallop, and Mowgli followed, thinking.

At any other season the news would have called all the Jungle together with bristling necks, but now they were busy hunting and fighting and killing and singing. From one to another Gray Brother ran, crying, "The Master of the Jungle goes back to Man! Come to the Council Rock." And the happy, eager People only answered, "He will return in the summer heats. The Rains will drive him to lair. Run and sing with us, Gray Brother."

"But the Master of the Jungle goes back to Man,"

Gray Brother would repeat.

"Eee — Yoawa? Is the Time of New Talk any less sweet for that?" they would reply. So when Mowgli, heavy-hearted, came up through the well-remembered rocks to the place where he had been brought into the Council, he found only the Four, Baloo, who was nearly blind with age, and the heavy, cold-blooded Kaa coiled around Akela's empty seat.

"Thy trail ends here, then, Manling?" said Kaa, as Mowgli threw himself down, his face in his hands. "Cry thy cry. We be of one blood, thou and I — man and snake together."

"Why did I not die under Red Dog?" the boy moaned. "My strength is gone from me, and it is not any poison. By night and by day I hear a double step upon my trail. When I turn my head it is as though one had hidden himself from me that instant. I go to look behind the trees and he is not there. I call and none cry again; but it is as though one listened and kept back the answer. I lie down, but I do not rest. I run the spring running, but I am not made still. I bathe, but I am not made cool. The kill sickens me, but I have no heart to fight except I kill. The Red Flower is in my body, my bones are water — and — I know not what I know."

"What need of talk?" said Baloo slowly, turning his head to where Mowgli lay. "Akela by the river said it, that Mowgli should drive Mowgli back to the Man-Pack. I said it. But who listens now to Baloo? Bagheera — where is Bagheera this night? — he knows also. It is the Law."

"When we met at Cold Lairs, Manling, I knew it," said Kaa, turning a little in his mighty coils. "Man goes to Man at the last, though the Jungle does not cast him out."

The Four looked at one another and at Mowgli,

puzzled but obedient.

"The Jungle does not cast me out, then?" Mowgli stammered.

Gray Brother and the Three growled furiously, beginning, "So long as we live none shall dare —" But Baloo checked them.

"I taught thee the Law. It is for me to speak," he said; "and, though I cannot now see the rocks before me, I see far. Little Frog, take thine own trail; make thy lair with thine own blood and pack and people; but when there is need of foot or tooth or eye, or a word carried swiftly by night, remember, Master of the Jungle, the Jungle is thine at call."

"The Middle Jungle is thine also," said Kaa. "I speak for no small people."

"Hai-mai, my brothers," cried Mowgli, throwing up his arms with a sob. "I know not what I know! I would not go; but I am drawn by both feet. How shall I leave these nights?"

"Nay, look up, Little Brother," Baloo repeated. "There is no shame in this hunting. When the honey is eaten we leave the empty hive."

"Having cast the skin," said Kaa, "we may not creep into it afresh. It is the Law."

"Listen, dearest of all to me," said Baloo. "There is neither word nor will here to hold thee back. Look up! Who may question the Master of the Jungle? I saw thee playing among the white pebbles yonder when thou wast a little frog; and Bagheera, that bought thee for the price of a young bull newly killed, saw thee also. Of that Looking Over we two only remain; for Raksha, thy lair-mother, is dead with thy lair-father; the old Wolf-Pack is long since dead; thou knowest whither Shere Khan went, and Akela died among the dholes, where, but for thy wisdom and strength, the second Seeonee Pack would also have died. There remains nothing but old bones. It is no longer the Man-cub that asks leave of his Pack, but the Master of the Jungle that changes his trail. Who shall question Man in his ways?"

"But Bagheera and the Bull that bought me," said Mowgli. "I would not —"

His words were cut short by a roar and a crash in the thicket below, and Bagheera, light, strong, and terrible as always, stood before him.

"Therefore," he said, stretching out a dripping right paw, "I did not come. It was a long hunt, but he lies dead in the bushes now — a bull in his second year — the Bull that frees thee, Little Brother. All debts are paid now. For the rest, my word is Baloo's word." He licked Mowgli's foot. "Remember, Bagheera loved thee," he cried, and bounded away. At the foot of the hill he cried again long and loud, "Good hunting on a new trail, Master of the Jungle! Remember, Bagheera loved thee."

"Thou hast heard," said Baloo. "There is no more. Go now; but first come to me. O wise Little Frog, come to me!"

"It is hard to cast the skin," said Kaa as Mowgli sobbed and sobbed, with his head on the blind bear's side and his arms round his neck, while Baloo tried feebly to lick his feet.

"The stars are thin," said Gray Brother, snuffing at the dawn wind. "Where shall we lair today? for from now, we follow new trails."

*A*nd this is the last of the Mowgli stories.

The Outsong

[This is the song that Mowgli heard behind him in the Jungle till he came to Messua's door again.]

Baloo

For the sake of him who showed
One wise Frog the Jungle-Road,
Keep the Law the Man-Pack make —
For thy blind old Baloo's sake!
Clean or tainted, hot or stale,
Hold it as it were the Trail,
Through the day and through the night,
Questing neither left nor right.
For the sake of him who loves
Thee beyond all else that moves,
When thy Pack would make thee pain,
Say: "Tabaqui sings again."
When thy Pack would work thee ill,
Say: "Shere Khan is yet to kill."
When the knife is drawn to slay,
Keep the Law and go thy way.
(Root and honey, palm and spathe,
Guard a cub from harm and scathe!)

Wood and Water, Wind and Tree,
Jungle-Favor go with thee!

Kaa

Anger is the egg of Fear —
Only lidless eyes are clear.
Cobra-poison none may leech.
Even so with Cobra-speech.
Open talk shall call to thee
Strength, whose mate is Courtesy.
Send no lunge beyond thy length;
Lend no rotten bough thy strength.
Gauge thy gape with buck or goat,
Lest thine eye should choke thy throat,
After gorging, wouldst thou sleep?
Look thy den is hid and deep,
Lest a wrong, by thee forgot,
Draw thy killer to the spot.
East and West and North and South,
Wash thy hide and close thy mouth.
(Pit and rift and blue pool-brim,
Middle-Jungle follow him!)
Wood and Water, Wind and Tree,
Jungle-Favor go with thee!

Bagheera

In the cage my life began;
Well I know the worth of Man.
By the Broken Lock that freed —
Man-cub, 'ware the Man-cub's breed!
Scenting-dew or starlight pale,
Choose no tangled tree-cat trail.
Pack or council, hunt or den,
Cry no truce with Jackal-Men.
Feed them silence when they say:
"Come with us an easy way."

Feed them silence when they seek
Help of thine to hurt the weak.
Make no banaar's boast of skill;
Hold thy peace above the kill.
Let nor call nor song nor sign
Turn thee from thy hunting-line.
(Morning mist or twilight clear,
Serve him, Wardens of the Deer!)
Wood and Water, Wind and Tree,
Jungle-Favor go with thee!

The Three
On the trail that thou must tread
To the thresholds of our dread,
Where the Flower blossoms red;
Through the nights when thou shalt lie
Prisoned from our Mother-sky,
Hearing us, thy loves, go by;
In the dawns when thou shalt wake
To the toil thou canst not break,
Heartsick for the Jungle's sake:
Wood and Water, Wind and Tree,
Wisdom, Strength, and Courtesy,
Jungle-Favor go with thee!

Printed in the United States
24109LVS00001B/292-300